KU-764-147

GRANTA BOOKS

THE IMAGINARY MONKEY

SEAN FRENCH

THE IMAGINARY MONKEY

GRANTA BOOKS
LONDON
in association with
PENGUIN BOOKS

GRANTA BOOKS
2/3 Hanover Yard, Noel Road, Islington, London N1 8BE
Published in association with the Penguin Group
Penguin Books Ltd, 27 Wrights Lane, London W8 5TZ, England
Viking Penguin, a division of Penguin Books USA Inc.,
375 Hudson Street, New York NY 10014, USA
Penguin Books Australia Ltd, Ringwood, Victoria, Australia
Penguin Books Canada Ltd, 2801 John Street, Markham,
Ontario, Canada L3R 1B4
Penguin Books (NZ) Ltd, 182–190 Wairau Road,
Auckland 10, New Zealand

Penguin Books Ltd, Registered Offices: Harmondsworth, Middlesex, England

First published by Granta Books 1993

1 3 5 7 9 10 8 6 4 2

Printed in Great Britain by Butler & Tanner Ltd, Frome and London

A CIP catalogue record for this book is available from the British Library

ISBN 014 014 233 9

To Nicci

If a lion could talk, we could not understand him.

Ludwig Wittgenstein

Does the Eagle know what is in the pit?
Or wilt thou go ask the Mole?

William Blake

PART ONE

THE REALM OF NECESSITY

I

IT SEEMS A long time ago and not to matter much anyway, but I believe it began with a rejection. Now rejections come in many forms, and sometimes it is hard to recognize them when they do. Writing is difficult for me, in a strictly physical sense at least, but let me describe an unambiguous example that comes from well before the beginning, when I was a boy of about eleven years of age.

It was one of the last weeks of the summer term of my first year at grammar school and it also must have been the last lesson of the day. Mr Lean, who was at that time my form teacher, asked me to stay behind and see him after school. If he had been born into my generation and been a woman and been a feminist, his is the sort of name that would have been changed to Leap as—what exactly is it?—I suppose a form of self-encouragement mingled with self-assertiveness. Certainly the name 'Lean' seemed to have defined every detail of that particular possessor in each of its senses. He was both frail and gaunt, his head as wrinkled as a peach stone, and his flesh browned as if it had been dried on a rock out in the sun. He was like an impermeable, tanned object, but then all teachers were objects to me. Occasionally, out kicking a ball around on a Saturday, I would see one of them at a distance, an animal strayed from its habitat. His clothes would be incongruously casual, and there might even be a stranger with him, a child or a partner of indeterminate gender, disconcertingly suggesting a life outside the school and the possibility of real emotions to go with it.

How did I react to being kept behind after school? I can't remember, but my end-of-day routine was inflexible. I put my text books, all obediently covered with sticky-backed plastic, in one side of my desk, and the exercise books, all identified by name, form and subject, in the other, then locked it with a frail unsatisfying click. One of the pleasing accessories of adulthood is the jingling bunch of keys, chunky and assertive in the pocket, attached to a battered leather toy or a miniature torch or the insignia of a car (the objects of human daily life possess a retrospective charm for me now). There will be a key to your front door and another for the mortice, others for the office, for the car or for the bicycle lock. When I was eleven I had not yet been entrusted even with a house key but I did have this key to my desk. In older days, when the distinction between *meum* and *tuum* was respected, such prophylaxes were not necessary, but now we all protected our unloved school books with a little hinged bolt screwed with a borrowed screwdriver at an uncomfortable angle to the clean underside of the desk where no one had ever bothered to write messages or inscribe a heart, an arrow or a cheerful obscenity.

Perhaps I then rested my worried brow on the cool surface of the desk, itself furrowed by years of gouging. All those generations of football teams and pop groups and forgotten names from primeval classes four or five years older than ourselves.

But I do remember what happened after the classroom had emptied and the rattles and yells faded. Our teacher had a thin voice that did not so much issue from his mouth as whistle weakly through it.

'Come here, Weaver.'

This use of surnames had been the greatest shock when I arrived at the school the previous September. It was one of the many affectations through which this school, inchoately sensible of its social inferiority, emulated what it thought it knew of public school life. The usage spread among new boys like the yearly epidemic of influenza, and soon old friends who had come together from primary school where they had been *tutoy*ing each other since they could speak were addressing each other with the newly assumed formality of Edwardian clubmen.

I advanced silently, clutching my plastic briefcase which I carried to and from school hollow except for sheets of paper and a school book or two. I assumed I had unwittingly infringed the school's Byzantine code of conduct. Or perhaps it was the recent end-of-year examinations; Mr Lean had marked our English language papers and awarded me a mark that even I—a vain small boy—could see was too high. I had anticipated that he might admit his mistake and strip me of the excess. Now I stood in front of the desk, its rim at my chin.

'No, come round here.'

I stepped up on to the dais and shuffled round, conscious that I was being permitted to peek behind the curtain at the Punch and Judy Show. This was what our class looked like from the exalted magisterial vantage point. Thirty empty echoing desks. Our first examination results were pinned to a cork notice-board.

'I like you, Weaver, do you know that?'

A teacher? Like? I felt a light pressure on my left shoulder, the one furthest from him. He had his arm round me. His ancient face was now just an inch or two from my own and I recall a tobacco aroma that pleasingly reminded me of my grandfather, who had recently died. I said nothing. I could think of nothing that could possibly be said.

'I like you very much.' His croak was almost unearthly, as if it had been squeezed from some extremity of his body, like a last splutter of toothpaste from a flattened tube. There was a final gasp.

'Do you like me?'

Some response was now required. As a matter of fact I

did like him, as much as I could like any of those automata who trundled in front of us during the hours of daylight before being shunted back to a shed somewhere. I was frightened of him of course, his unimaginable age, his air of having suffered. He had been stretched across something too far and too thinly. But I liked him well enough.

'No,' I said brightly, listening to my own voice with an almost scientific curiosity. Where did that word come from? What a terrible thing to say to a teacher. How did I dare?

'Very well, you can go now.'

As I turned to go he gave me a gentle slap on the behind. Or perhaps I should say, he longingly touched the firm, hairless buttocks of a small boy still unconscious of his own body. Once I grew up I was not to be, as I will explain, delicately framed, but as a pre-pubescent boy I was delicate enough. Attractive in a way.

Was this a rejection? At the time I didn't perceive it to be so. It seemed like a rude rebuff on my part to a civil offer of friendship; a callous brushing aside of an attempt to offer a hand across an unbridgeable gap. I didn't know why I had said what I had said, or even if there was a why to be discovered. The following Monday morning, when we filed into class to find the deputy headmaster waiting to tell us that Mr Lean had died over the weekend, there were various responses. One boy, now an executive in a failing jewellery company, sobbed and told me that it was the first time anyone actually known to him had died. Within ten years this boy's father, a massively robust wall of a man, red-faced, a sportsman, would also be dead, suddenly gone from a heart attack. Other boys laughed, one because he had failed to finish his homework over the weekend. Did I feel guilty that I had been rude to this old and feeble man *in extremis*? Was I puzzled by my apparently supernatural power?

The result of this brief encounter—at my end, anyway—was that I was a little less of a human being, unwilling, perhaps, to trust my immediate impulses. Like a hit and run driver, I never told anyone what had happened, fearing I might be blamed for the death. At first I thought I could be expelled, or even arrested and sent to Borstal, but then gradually the episode faded into one of those semi-dormant memories that can be pulled out of the stacks and always relied upon to deliver a muted shock, like the terminal of an old battery that can still impart a reminiscent tingle to the exploratory tip of the tongue.

II

I SEE MYSELF on the whole less as a rejector than as a rejectee. It's true, I have resigned from one or two bodies. I remember once leaving a book club before I had bought my statutory three titles, and I never kept up the membership dues for my school's Old Boys society. These, however, are exceptions. More indelible is the memory of letters I received—manila envelopes containing a single sheet, sometimes addressed to Dear Sir or Madam, sometimes with my own name written in at the top; coloured envelopes crammed with bulky stacks of paper covered with yards of tortured spidery writing—the contents of which only added up to a long N-O.

Less often it happens face to face. It has been my experience of the occasional employment that I have undertaken over the years that you have lunch twice with your boss, excluding the terrible joviality of the Christmas lunches which everyone is dragooned into attending. I mean head to head encounters. The first is the occasion on which you are offered the job; the second is the occasion on which you are dismissed from it. If you are in possession of a job and your employer invites you to have lunch, then it is likely to be the second rather than the first form of lunch that is in prospect. Although this does not always hold true. I once had lunch with an employer during which I was offered another, better, job. I turned it down, replying that I was quite happy with the first job, thank you very much. I was then sacked from the first job, without the benefit of another lunch. The information arrived in a manila envelope.

It is easy to postulate rules, less easy to recognize them when they manifest themselves in the course of quotidian existence. On another occasion I was invited to lunch by a female employer. The nature of my job at the time seems unimportant to me now; I can scarcely conceive what it might have been. I ought simply to have applied the Weaver litmus test. We have had one lunch. Hence this is inevitably the second and valedictory one. But I didn't. And I'm afraid that among the possibilities I canvassed was the notion that my employer might be sexually attracted to me.

This was extremely unlikely. I have portrayed the young Gregory Weaver as a type familiar to those of us of post-child-abuse age: a slight, hairless, pretty thing likely to be preyed on by the unscrupulous old. I even feel a slight stir myself looking at that svelte figure in the Man. United kit, right foot proudly poised atop the tan leather soccer ball. What has happened to my short-term memory? I can recall every detail from thirty years ago. I remember that ball when we played in the rain, which we always seemed to do, turning into a sodden bean bag. Heading it was like kissing a soggy upper-cut.

But I was now far from svelte. I no longer have access to old photographs, but I doubt whether the sight of me in my late twenties would elicit anything except disgust. I was going through a bad patch and I had let myself go. The dissipation and neglect which look so attractive in the movies had done little for me. Since puberty I had been a fat person in a world of the disapproving thin. While others scourged themselves, I had nurtured the image of myself as a priapic Jack Falstaff, with a suggestion of the decadent excess of a Roman emperor. But people just thought I ate and smoked too much and took no exercise, or that I had something wrong with my glands. Raising my body out of a chair became an effort. Narrowing my eyes was perceptibly easier. I wanted someone to mother me, and indeed there was by that time an urgent need for someone to do for me the things that mothers do for their children, such as washing them, brushing their hair and buying them clothes that fit.

Despite my amnesia as regards almost anything to do with clothes, I can remember what Susan (no second names by this time) was wearing that day. She had on a soft creamy wool dress, of the sort that seems to invite the onlooker to stroke it and offer the creature inside a lump of sugar. It reached halfway down her stockinged legs, and the top folded over in an exaggerated turtle-neck, like the ruffed out feathers of a cockatoo. A cockatoo doing a courtship dance, I thought to myself, wrongly. Her dark brown hair had a stiff curliness; it looked as if it might crumble in your fingers. Her face was not beautiful but it was closely attended to in a way that I found very—what word am I looking for?—something like intriguing or involving. It was not just the effect of the black lines applied to every traceable contour of the eye-sockets, or the sharp-edged precision of the pouting red lips. It was her skin, which was powdered with an intensive thoroughness that I generally associated with women of the era of my late grandmother. I've never quite understood what this powder is for—in my grandmother's case its purpose seemed to be to dry up the skin in readiness for the nightly daubing from the cold cream bucket—but on Susan's face the result was that every pore, every hair, stood out as if sprinkled with a fine coating of synthetic snow. A pedant might have observed that the powder resulted in a pallor that demanded compensating artificial colour. But its effect, making her look both very alive and very dead, was not unpleasing.

It must have taken her so long to get ready. All that care and attention just to have lunch with me, I thought, even though I knew that she never *didn't* look as if she were on her way to some event on the social ladder many rungs above me. I settled down at the table and began to gnaw on one of those long, thin, deeply unsatisfying Italian biscuity bread things. We were at a local restaurant, called *Il trittico* or *Il elbow*, or a name of that kind, and I looked through the menu for something big. For a first course I ordered ravioli stuffed with a lot of ingredients and then, to follow, a slice of beef served raw with slices of cheese, lemon juice, potatoes and courgettes. My bottle of red wine arrived in a basket. Susan ordered a mixed salad as a main course and a bottle of mineral water.

This was a bad sign. Once, at a time when I cared frantically about such things, I read an article in a sleazy magazine or tabloid newspaper that purported to identify a mode of behaviour that suggests a couple's mutual attraction in the early stages of courtship. If there is such an attraction, then they start, unconsciously, to imitate each other's posture. I don't remember whether attraction could actually be generated by deliberately imitating the posture of your partner, or whether this would be counter-productive. Nor do I remember whether other actions apart from body posture were significant. But as our orders diverged, I began to have an ominous feeling, like a besieged chess player who senses that his position is indefensible but cannot quite tell from where the attack will come.

And so, I remember every detail of that awful lunch. She wore cream, I wore one of my terrible indistinguishable old jackets. The waiter brandished a pepper grinder that was about three feet long. I can't reconstruct the bits of gossip which, joined together in rudimentary fashion, formed makeshift conversation. But even the gossip wasn't real gossip. It was worse than that. To provide me with gossip would have been, from Susan's point of view, to inject valuable funds into a company that, unknown to itself, was trading illegally.

I picked at my meal. That is, I *ought* to have picked at it. But with a huge slice of beef, however much you are trying to show sullen dignity, you still need to chomp, tear and munch with carnivorous zeal simply to dispose of it, an activity that comes to seem ignominious, if not obscene, when performed under the eyes of someone you've forgotten is a vegetarian and who is also about to fire you.

'How are you enjoying it?'

She did have a wonderfully, almost parodically silky voice, the sort that belongs to someone lying on a rug next to a log fire in a commercial selling something designed for bachelors.

'It's a bit chewy, but it's all right really. The lemon juice cooks it apparently, so it doesn't really count as raw.'

'I'm sorry, I meant your work.'

Fuck. She had been continuing a conversation that had begun inside her head, where she had been practising different ways of broaching the subject. Better to have done it at the end of the meal, really. Or by post. I wondered what to say. I had to behave with dignity. It was like being taken to the electric chair. Once the warders have come to get you, you must go quietly and not embarrass everyone. (Or should one scream and cry and hold on to the bars of the cell just to show everyone that a human being like them is being cruelly put to death?)

The slim possibility occurred to me that she had not finally made up her mind. If she had made up her mind, it might seem more dignified if I said that it wasn't going very well and now that she mentioned it, I had decided to hand in my notice and she would be receiving a letter to that effect in the morning. On the other hand if she hadn't, then the best tactic would be to claim that it was all going very well indeed. If I were robust enough in my assertion of how terrifically successful I considered myself to be, perhaps it might change her mind. But did I really want to struggle on in a job where I wasn't really wanted? And what if I was wanted after all and I had misread the meal from beginning to end? After all nothing had actually been said either to confirm or deny my hopes or apprehension. Perhaps she was making conversation and she really did lust after me? Perhaps . . .

'I'm afraid I don't think it's really worked out.'

That was Susan talking, not me. I never got a chance to make any of my various interventions. I couldn't think of anything to say. I still couldn't think of anything but now I had to say something.

'How do you mean?'

'I don't think it's really working.'

She looked down into her still mineral water. The conversation had already degenerated into a meaningless game. The message had already been written down and pushed through my metaphorical letterbox. I was now handing it back to the postman so that he could push it through the box once more, perhaps with the picture side of the card up so that it would look more pleasing, although the message would be no different. I was a headless chicken disputing the means of its execution. As usual I could think of plenty of useless comparisons but I seemed to have no artillery at my disposal.

There is a legal maxim that a barrister should only ask a question of a witness if he knows what answer he is going to receive. If I asked Susan why she felt the way she did, she might honestly tell me what the problem was, or she might tell me something that would make her feel better, or she might tell me something that she thought might make me feel better. Even if she were honest, and there would be no way of telling if she had been, I didn't care what her reasons happened to be. The fact of our relationship was that she had power and I didn't. Detached from her authority, her opinions were of no interest to me.

She still appeared to be waiting for an answer, for some sort of response, something that would validate her judgement. For all I knew, she wanted me to break down and beg, or to get angry so that the conversation could turn into a confrontation. More likely she wanted the sort of handshake that boys give to their master in school stories when they have been flogged for their own good. Hegel said that the criminal has a right to his punishment, that it is an acknowledgement of his freedom. But how would Hegel have reacted to being sacked across a lunch table? It wasn't that I was intent on denying her any satisfaction. I already had other things on my mind. There was the amount of money in my current account, my deposit account and my building society account added together and roughly divided by the rent on my room. I was also pondering how this humiliation could best be redeemed in the telling. Evasively—'I thought it was time to move on.' Baldly—'I was sacked.' Dishonestly—'I resigned on a matter of principle.' What had to be avoided above all, even in the last extremity, was the appearance of conflict. I had to go for charm.

'Oh well.' This was really me talking. 'Am I still allowed pudding?'

'Yes, of course.'

There was a rattle of relieved laughter. I felt for a moment like an aristocrat on the scaffold, a benedictory hand on the trembling head of the executioner. I imagined that I was making her feel better when I was really preventing myself from feeling anything at all. We kept up the appearance of being friends, though if I ever saw her drowning or lying in the street with an artery severed, I would just walk by pretending not to notice. I looked at the menu once more, in its stupid Italian. Zabaglione, for two persons only. I ordered both of them for myself and then two cups of coffee and finished off the chianti while a small man in my head did the talking for both of us.

III

ALL OF WHICH is delaying the story. I find myself dwelling with a distant fascination on these joustings that make up human inter-relations. But it is this story I intend to tell, this story that I am writing covertly in the small hours of the night, in premises not my own, on paper I have stolen from various sources so that it will not be missed, gripping my pen painfully like a toddler clutching a crayon in a hand not designed for the task. And what about the design of my brain? I don't know.

This is the story of how Susan rejected me. Not the Susan who sacked me; this is another Susan altogether. It might have helped if they had had different names but life is like that sometimes. They didn't, they had the same name. It might even have made a difference if I had known one of them as Sue or Susie, or by a nickname, like Bobo or Snuffle, but I didn't. And it's not as if there were no other rejectors to choose from. There is a whole directory, not just of girl's names—Jane, Liz, Eva, Emmie, admittedly yet another Susan, what chance synaptic network of my brain is charged by, masochistically attracted to, those two syllables?—but also of educational institutions, trustees of scholarships and other voluntary funds, employers. But the antagonist of this story is unavoidably Susan. The first one, the employer, won't be mentioned again. The second's role in my life is too trivial to be worth mentioning. The third and final Susan, the ultimate rejector, is Susan Gower.

To you, whoever you are, holding these indistinct scratchings in your hands, those are for the moment just words. Susan Gower. If you could feel what I once felt, tracing the curves and angles of that name, well, then my task would be virtually complete. But even I no longer feel it, I no longer need to feel it. Invocations are archaic but I feel that I need some form of aid. Not from a muse, but perhaps from Ovid's gods, those who have wrought every change. I remember that well enough. Or more appropriately still, Circe, the woman who turns men into beasts, can you guide my hairy and unsteady hand?

First meetings of lovers are meant to be charming. There is even a phrase for the way that the plot in Hollywood films causes people to meet each other by crashing their cars, by one knocking the other into a swimming pool, by the girl being arrested by the man who happens to be a policeman, and so on: *meeting cute.* I've never heard much of it in real life. Meeting ugly would be the more fitting term. I was once at a party, talking with a group that was made up of a few married couples. One grinning husband started asking people in a light bantering sort of way how they and their partners had met. People looked into their drinks and produced anodyne little anecdotes.

'And how did you meet?' I asked him, assuming that the subject had been raised as a pretext for him to tell their own amusing story. He gave his wife a nervous smile. I was on the dangerous third martini and boisterously urged them on.

'Come on, it must be something funny.'

A humorous response was now called for and the wife spoke with a smile that looked as if it had been strained painfully through her face.

'We first met when Bill was married to my sister.'

The nasty interior details of other people's lives are so fascinating. People are so dull and correct and sane when you meet them, so apparently in control of their world. But if you could get into their homes and rifle through their drawers, be a fly on the wall during their mutual recriminations, overhear their goatish confessions, eavesdrop at the VD clinic, squeeze under the couch or behind the pillow for those post-coital intimacies, *then* they would suddenly become characters worth knowing.

When I first met Susan what we had in common was that I was living in a madhouse and she was going mad, and neither of us was looking for a sexual partner. If we had been, then neither of us would have chosen the other. But she changed me, she changed me in various ways—of that there is no doubt. I altered her as well. But I'm already doing too much analysis—that was always my problem. Life is a matter of maintaining oneself between contradictions that can't be resolved by analysis, someone once said. That was what it felt like, though 'maintaining' may be too purposeful a word for what we went through. I can't say I understand what happened, but let me just describe a few bits of it, not even the skeleton of an affair but a few discrete bones, a stray sternum, a fragment of skull, a tibia, a thigh bone, which when partially assembled might give some sense of the way the original creature looked when it walked, haltingly, close to extinction, on the earth.

This was in the second half of the eighties. In the events that follow I was on the slope that swept me past the thirty barrier and out to sea. I was looking older by this time, though I had not yet hit rock bottom or anything like it. But the safety net was beginning to leave its mark on me, criss-crossed on my pale flesh. I, a person whose whole existence was dedicated to the avoidance of conflict, was now living in a cavernous and dark south London house presided over by a woman who banged at doors and screamed in the middle of the night and vomited in any of the sinks to which she could gain access. Other tenants would move in and move out on the same evening but the arrangements suited me. Dear Vera was paranoid and without a short-term memory. Consequently, after a trial period of two months I discovered that her mood remained the same whether I paid the rent or not and so I did not. My L-shaped room was right at the top of the house, forming its top storey, light enough, with windows both front and back, and with a stout lock on the door. Admittedly this made entering or leaving the house a particular challenge, forcing me to run, or mount, a gauntlet of three long flights of stairs, but the verbal contract between Vera and me remained an arrangement of mutual convenience that left both of us unhappy but me closer to solvency than I had been for some years.

At an advanced stage of this tenure, when the poltergeist of Jude Avenue was growing intolerable even for me, I was sitting at a pavement café with an acquaintance watching the passing traffic. This last word I use in its traditional mechanical sense. We were not, after all, in Nice but in a particularly charmless London high street. I had always wanted to have a friend who was fat like me, but such a friend is hard to find and my companion of that morning, called Pedro, though he claimed to be Danish, was a vegan, spectacularly thin and very unhealthy indeed. He eschewed almost anything that most of us would consider to be food, subsisting instead on cigarettes and black coffee. I had probably made some sombre, sweeping statement about the river of humanity that was rolling past us when Pedro pointed across the road.

'See that woman over there, the one in the anorak? What sort of person do you think she is?'

IV

I STARED AT the woman over the road. She was standing in the queue at the bank machine, and seemed to be talking to herself.

'She's got glasses, so she can probably read. She hasn't brushed her hair, she looks like she's slept in her clothes. She must be a mental patient who's been released back into the community. She lives in a halfway house where she's probably abused on a regular basis.'

'All right, you can stop that. She's a friend of mine.' Pedro whistled across the road and summoned her over. They kissed with a click of spectacle frames.

It's not really an exact account of the occasion on which I first met Susan. The story was to become one of my turns—of the how-we-first-met variety—and so embellished and lengthened that I can't remember exactly what happened. There were versions that went on for ten minutes, where I inferred a whole history of deprivation and squalor, vividly, even obscenely, evoked. That would have been funnier, but in reality I don't think I got a chance to venture any opinion at all before Pedro the Dane summoned her over and introduced us, me as a man who lived in a flat he didn't dare go back to, and her as a woman who had spent five years working on a thesis that she was never going to finish.

I can't remember a word she said at that meeting. She probably talked to Pedro—can it *really* have been Pedro? I think my memory for names has been the first to go. Perhaps it was Peter, or even something plausibly Danish, like Per. But the impressions that mattered remain clear. She had a build I approved of, big like a country girl. As I later discovered, she was five foot ten inches tall, a full inch above me. And her greyish brown hair wasn't unkempt, as I'd first thought, but long and striking in its way. I've heard that if you don't wash hair then after a time it starts to clean itself by some improbable biological process. I've no idea if this is true. It certainly wasn't true of my own shiny strands which had been left to themselves over the years, and Susan never put the theory into practice. She spent much of our time together crouched over a sink foamily kneading her scalp. But her hair looked the way that I imagined self-cleaning, self-combing hair would look if it got itself together and took some responsibility.

Susan wore tortoiseshell glasses but she didn't look like a student. I couldn't imagine her sitting in a college library taking notes from books that weren't designed to be read. She looked more like a manual labourer. Her hands were rough and calloused, her nails bitten down below the tips of her stubby fingers. Bitten down to the quick is the usual expression, and I had always confused the word, for some reason, with the cuticle, and pictured ferociously neurotic adolescents consuming their own stumpily bloody fingers. There was nothing neurotic about Susan's auto-ingestion, in which she also nibbled at the skin around the corner of each nail. It was more like an absent-minded sign of approval.

Her cheeks were red, almost flushed, as if she had been out since dawn reaping and gleaning in the fields. Was she beautiful, or even pretty? I don't know about things like that, certainly not any more, but I remember that from the very moment she sat down with a theatrical sigh on the tinny, perforated chair, she looked at home in her body, lucky woman.

I was also struck by something she said. The Dane (if he actually was Danish, he may have been Norwegian or even German, I never knew him particularly well, and Susan once even went so far as to claim that I had first met him through her, which must be wrong) started a conversation about the fur trade—one of those eating-people-is-wrong issues on which all right-thinking people agree, and even if they do not would never dare say so.

'I'm not pretending that it's black and white,' Per said. 'But the fact that there are grey areas doesn't mean . . . ' He cast around for what it might not mean. 'That you'd ever wear a fur coat. There are limits.'

Susan was dressed in jeans and a jeans jacket that didn't match and which a bulky amber sweater underneath made impossible to close or even to pull together.

'I'd love a fur coat,' she said. 'Just the thing.'

I am now constitutionally opposed to any use of animals by man but even back then I was pretty much a vegetarian except for eating fish and a bit of meat occasionally. I wasn't going to go on a demonstration or raid a laboratory or anything like that but I was certainly against things like fox-hunting and fur coats and experiments on fluffy animals to make things that I didn't buy. But I thought that there was something adorable about her saying 'I'd love a fur coat.' It was the very pointlessness of it. It seemed extremely unlikely that she would ever get a fur coat, and if she had been tempted seriously to tout for one then Pedro and I were the poorest of prospects. That Saturday morning wasn't even of the cold variety that might stir thoughts of furry comfort. It was warm and muggy in preparation for getting more so. Her 'Just the thing' was a pure expression of self-pleasuring, the self-indulgent enjoyment of something that had been stripped off the flesh of some once-furry animal or other, perhaps one that was a member of an endangered species. I could picture her winding it round her body, the collar turned up into her neck, hugging herself.

The next time we met was the result of a misunderstanding on my part that is far too complicated to explain and not really relevant anyway. The result was that I found myself once more at the café referred to above while my intended companion was at a restaurant in another part of London which I had never heard of before but which had a slightly similar name to the café. By five to one I had read the menu and ordered a beer. At one o'clock my face assumed an appropriately expectant expression. By ten past the expression had become strained and I was starting to wish I had brought something to read. By twenty past my carefully rationed beer was almost gone and I was feeling out of place among the conversations taking place around me between friends flushed with the achievements of a morning's shopping. Facing with dismay a social abyss, I jumped at a coarse tap on my shoulder.

'You don't look quite the ticket.'

'Oh, hello. It's Susan, isn't it? I'm waiting for someone.'

'She must have found someone better. Come and join us.'

Susan was sitting with a man wearing a neatly pressed donkey jacket. He ought to have taken it off when he arrived, and he knew it, but it was too late now. His hair was cut short with great care, he was slim, tastefully fashionable and, I thought, quite startlingly handsome. He was obviously cross at my presence, but gave a polite smile of welcome as I shuffled along the pinewood bench and sat down next to him, opposite Susan.

'Go and get yourself a salad,' said Susan. 'And I'll have a coffee. What do you want, Kit?'

Kit wanted a coffee as well. I found myself with a salad made out of walnuts and slices of fruit. I may have put vinaigrette on a pudding by mistake but I didn't mind. It was a perfect social occasion.

I should explain.

For Kit, whom I didn't know and never met again, it was a bit of a disaster, of which he was plainly aware, but on the other hand he was suddenly relieved of the need to entertain and could assume the role of the self-righteously aggrieved, smoking cigarettes and staring into his coffee. Susan, who had been previously stuck with the responsibility of cranking a cold, spluttery, coughing conversation into motion, was now manipulating two men with a cheerfully mischievous irresponsibility. It wasn't exactly *Jules and Jim*, to give the film its English title, but power is a drug even in small doses.

And I felt myself the principal beneficiary of chance. Sky a ball in my direction at the climax of my first Test Match in front of the world's television cameras and I'll fumble it. Toss it to me on a beach and I may well hang on. If I had arranged to meet Susan and had had time to prepare things to say that might impress her, we would have become perfectly correct acquaintances, kissing each other on the cheeks, exchanging information, but frankly not all that interested. We would have missed out entirely on the chance to damage each other as only the closest friends can do. The prospect of lunch with Susan and the morose Kit would have been an ordeal, but now it was my escape from an hour of sitting alone in a noisy health food restaurant, wondering how long I could prevent people from placing their trays down opposite me. I wouldn't go so far as to assert that I sparkled with my witty conversation, or that the true lovable depths of my personality were revealed. It's just that for a rare hour I resembled a normal human being, just when Susan was in the mood to meet one.

When I was younger and baffled by the rituals of the human species, I used to wonder what one had to say in order to make a girl be attracted to one. No, let me rephrase that in more behaviourist language. Which acts and signals in what sequence would result in lips being applied to lips, the removal of clothing, the fondling of parts of the body and the unimaginable penetration itself? I knew very well what the initial stage was: a girl whom you hardly knew at all. And I had a febrile sense of what the final stage was: all the normal barriers that ruled my life gone; an entirely naked girl letting me do what I wanted to her within limits that I could imagine were in themselves exciting. But what got you from one to the other?

I'd see a fat boy on the tube with his arm awkwardly encircling a fat girl, or I'd see a male and a female down-and-out slouched in a corner asleep, a bottle of cooking sherry wedged between them, and I would ask myself with an aggrieved sense of betrayal, what exactly did he say to her which resulted in her agreeing to be held by him? Which areas of the brain need to be stimulated in order to provoke a particular emotional response? I never tried to answer the question by considering which areas of my brain responded to the requisite prodding from without. But then girls were different from me, they needed to be deluded into sexual attraction; I didn't believe that they actually felt it.

I still didn't understand the workings of my own brain. The content of what Susan said that lunch-time didn't matter at all. I'd liked the archness of her expression and the set of her jaw when she said she'd like a fur coat. I'd been charmed, I'd been in the mood to be charmed, by the way she thumped me on the back—'not quite the ticket', where had she got that ridiculous expression from?—and by the way she had bullied me into changing tables, which had also been a way of needling Kit. It was as if I had now made a purely intellectual decision to approve of her. I was not in love with her; I had not said, even to myself, that I liked or was attracted to her; yet I was in a strange phase of finding everything she did surprising and adorable. So from then on, though this phase was to last a relatively short time, it didn't matter what she said or did. I was determined to like it, whatever it was.

Once you have decided that someone is bewitching, she becomes bewitching under your endorsing gaze. I knew this because I had suffered from the consequences of the opposing rule, according to which once a partner has decided that everything you do is foolish and contemptible, you begin to live down to her expectations, a doomed straight man to a disapproving straight woman. The observations are trite, the jokes are stale, the car stalls with the humiliating *duh-duh-duh* forward motion, the film you choose is unenjoyably awful, it rains. In those circumstances there are no buttons left to press, except for the eject button.

What did we actually talk about? Susan teased me about mixing up appointments, and of course my inability to be in the right place at the right time suddenly seemed like an endearing quality to be dramatized and nurtured. She in turn then talked skittishly about her hopeless years of research on an author who was neglected when she began but was now an academic cliché on whom careers were being made, though not hers. Suddenly her failure seemed enchanting. I gave a satirical account of the decay of my lodgings and my landlady, which I had long ceased to find anything but harrowing, but even Kit grinned as I mimicked the nodding of unrecognition as I passed Mrs Dean on the stairs and rapped on the stripped pine table in imitation of the frenzied knocks on my door that I would ignore.

I would later discover that the pressures of Susan's academic work had driven her to a half-serious suicide attempt (she would never tell me the exact details but it was pills, I think, and provoked by work problems, another man, a grey winter) and she was never again quite so fond of my unreliability with appointments, or indeed anything else about me, but we were not thinking of the future as lunch-time turned into afternoon, and the café gradually emptied.

V

I DRIBBLED THE last of the whisky into a glass retrieved from the bathroom.

'I'll have this one, since you never know who might have puked up into it.'

Susan was drinking her tablespoonful of whisky from a wine glass, otherwise used for storing pencils, and taking the last cigarette from a packet which had been opened a couple of hours earlier.

A fortnight had passed since Susan, Kit and I had had lunch. In the meantime, Susan had had her hair cut drastically so that she looked like an urban terrorist. I had escorted her up the stairs to my penthouse (no sign of Mrs Bates) and after she had taken her coat off I saw that she had done things to herself. There were definite signs of make-up around her eyes and mouth. I felt myself unqualified to comment on the result, but it was the fact that she had done it that made me shiver. For half an hour or so she had fiddled with her face in front of the mirror because of the prospect of spending an evening with me.

She was dressed in the same jeans and anonymous mannish shirt that I had seen before but over it—this was 1988, remember—was an intricate coloured waistcoat. I wondered what it would be like to take it off. Although this evening was destined ultimately to be a failure on my part, it would also prove to be the most exciting, the most simply interesting, we would ever spend together. There were plenty of later occasions that were better in different ways, more enjoyable, but this was the evening when we found ourselves at the station deciding which train to board. Stations are stressful places—cases to be hauled around, timetables to be consulted, absurd waiting, unintelligible signals, the anxiety about being on the right platform and even on the right train—but at least a station is a place of change. On more tranquil, more successful occasions in the future, we were just on the train, passively accepting the ride.

Some music. I riffled through the LPs which were leaning against the end of the sofa.

'What would you like?'

'I think the idea is to put on some soft music and then make coffee for us both.'

The waft of intoxication and flirtatiousness hung in the air the way that incense used to, in the days when people lit incense on occasions such as these. Susan had not, in the few conversations we had had, ever said explicitly in any way that she liked or desired me, but I suspected that she would never be attracted to me more than in the hazy, pretty undiscriminating way she was at the moment. God, this was sexier than any sex could ever be. I ran my finger from right to left along the row of slim spines. Those old names, the ones that had escaped the one-way journey to the second-hand shop. Zoo Station. The Yachts. The X-Dreamysts. The Wasps. The Vipers. The Undertones. The Tours. The Shapes. The Radio Stars. Q Tips. The Piranhas. Original Mirrors. Names. The Moondogs. The Lurkers. King. The Icicle Works. Homme de Terre. The Glaxo Babies. The Flys. Essential Logic. The Distractions. The Cravats. The Birthday Party. The Au-Pairs. Where were they now, with their thinning hair and expired contracts? I chose a jazz record that I had never listened to, but it had a moody cover and seemed safely old and neutral. I sucked the last of the whisky through clenched teeth. It stung the soft roots where they had been left exposed by the recession of my gums. I wasn't even thirty. Within five years I'd have nothing but a mouthful of dry bone.

'Is the door locked?'

I felt an excited constriction inside my chest as if a small rodent were trying to climb from my stomach into my oesophagus.

'Yes, and anyway there's no sign of Mrs Bates. She must be down in the cellar in her rocking chair.'

'I thought she was called Mrs Dean.' One of the first things I loved about Susan was that she knew absolutely nothing about the cinema.

When you find yourself in the situation in which I was now finding myself, there is a variety of things you can do. The first, which I realized I had adopted unwittingly for a number of years, is to claim illness or simply ignore all signals, and either swiftly call a halt to the evening or allow it to drift, slowly and painfully, into nothingness. You will then feel, possibly for the rest of your life, one of the more painful varieties of *l'esprit de l'escalier*, that sense of something that ought to have been said or done. The second is to initiate a series of imperceptibly escalating contacts, the earliest of which are apparently inadvertent, providing a tacit approach which can tacitly be rejected with no apparent embarrassment. But perhaps this strategy is more offensive rather than less. By not taking a direct approach, the man retains the possibility of persuading himself, when he is rejected, that the invitation was all in the woman's mind; he had made no advances, could not therefore have been rejected, and the woman obviously wanted a fuck anyway. A gentleman would make the invitation explicit, and accept the embarrassment that would come with any rejection. There is something peculiarly English about this particular style. A French woman once told me of the awkwardness of having to reject an invitation that, it was then claimed, had not even been offered. But as I write this I wonder if when she told me all this, she was herself making a form of invitation, thus refuting her own argument? Well, I'm beyond all that now.

A third method is, as I have said, to make the invitation explicit. This, I must confess, I have never tried, but I understand it usually involves words such as, 'Would you like to stay?'—as if this were just another routine transaction, by which no mature adult could be embarrassed. But again, the explicit approach itself contains an element of presumably deliberate ambiguity. 'Stay over' might suggest that what is being offered is a sexless spare room. Simply 'stay' means that sex is almost certainly on offer, but there can be a shift in meaning at a late stage if necessary.

There is a host of other possibilities, of course, some of which involve violence. My own approach was direct, even, for me at least, impulsive. I placed my glass on the desk by the door. I sat down on Susan's right side and took her glass from her right hand, her cigarette from between the fingers of her left hand and, in a gesture of some aplomb, stubbed the latter out in the former, with a slight hiss. The hiss came from the cigarette, not from me.

I don't want anyone to misunderstand this. The reader may consider me cold-blooded for not pushing my lips against the lit cigarette or letting the glass spill its contents on Susan's only pair of trousers. Through my changed circumstances, I have a particular interest in breaking down the details of human interaction. When I look back on these events they seem emotional enough. But the overriding necessity in moments of apparent spontaneity is to act with precision. If the actor playing Hamlet becomes so emotional that he drops his foil and forgets his lines, then, instead of weeping for him, our interest will shift to the mechanics of stagecraft, an interesting matter but a different one, and appropriate for a different sort of theatre which has its own theoretical basis. There is such a thing as pure, utterly spontaneous impulse, but its practitioners are in prison or more likely in secure mental hospitals, generally with open-ended sentences.

Quite deliberately, looking her straight in the eye and trying not to smirk, I held her face in my hands, the index fingers touching the top of each cheekbone. She had a face like a mask; her features seemed oversized, yet, for that very reason, they were strangely harmonious. I thought it magnificent. There was no need to delay further. I leant forward and did not so much kiss her as touch her lips with mine, once and then again. The pressure increased and the sudden wet shock of her tongue reminded me that someone else was involved. I saw that the edge of her cheek visible through the lens of her spectacles appeared fractured from the rest, like a spoon in a glass of water. What big brown eyes she would have when the spectacles were removed.

On the relatively few occasions that I went through this process, a certain number of perceptions used to strike me. The first would occur to me at this stage, the moment of the first real kiss. I was always conscious that one friendship, or at least one form of one friendship, was now irretrievably gone and I must now—in an unreliable, almost deranged, state—face a relationship of a different order. I was an Alice who had drunk from an unknown bottle and stumbled blindly through a new doorway, which might not lead to a garden at all but directly out on to the motorway.

If this were a movie aimed at a family audience, there would now doubtless be a discreet circular panning shot revealing details of my life through the decorations of my room. Leaving Susan's left cheek, shoulder and the hand which was coming up to my face the camera would move along the sofa past the net-curtained window giving out on to the street and turn right at the wall. The wall would be adorned with significant, perhaps ironic, family photographs, stiff Victorian patriarchs attended by grave Sikh retainers, looking down on the sexual congress that was being initiated below. There was in reality no decoration on that wall except for a poster of the white windmills of Mykonos which had belonged to the previous tenant, a woman who had been disappointed in love, according to the report of her ex-landlady in a lucid moment.

Turning right again brings us to the door, locked and also bolted, to guard against even the use of Mrs Dean's own key. Then matters become more interesting with my desk, on which was a typewriter in which was a single sheet of an unfinished article on box-folding which I was writing for a technical magazine. Also piled on the desk was the customary pile of unanswered mail and beside that, more poignantly, my box of white A4 typing paper, which could be considered my pile of unwritten mail, articles and fiction, though this would be difficult to convey in a single shot. We then reach another corner and the receding stroke of the L which took the room to the back window of the house. On the left of this recess was my bed, with a new sheet and the duvet pulled back casually so as not to look too much like a baited trap. On the right was a dark and gloomy wardrobe of the type that can be found in every rented property of a certain age in the kingdom. Turning right once more brings us to the television and the VCR. Then the fireplace. On the mantelpiece were a couple of invitations—a close-up might reveal that they were both yellowed archaic relics.

In a movie, the camera would then linger over the flames licking and caressing the logs, symbolizing the fires of passion. But this is not, or not yet, a movie, and, as is traditional in rented accommodation, the fireplace had long been boarded up. The gas fire which had replaced it was switched on—at a low level, this was still summer—but it scarcely had the same symbolic effect. So the camera carries on moving, turning right before coming to the second window. Below the window is the record player, its stylus wobbling on the first side of *Kind of Blue.* We then pass the serried ranks of the Weaver record collection, left to right, then rise slightly to skim the sofa's edge and return to Susan and me.

After enough mutual tonguing to demonstrate passion, I pulled back and kissed her lightly on the upper and lower lip, nibbling the latter slightly. I hoped this would express a mixture of abandon, affection and respect. We were both adults, consent seemed to be implied and it was time to take her clothes off. This can generally be done while kissing but the action is somehow more exciting when performed with the same gravity that anticipated the first kiss. I decided to leave her tortoiseshell glasses where they were. One of us needed to be able to see what was going on. I undid the buttons of her waistcoat, which took a surprisingly long time. Only buffoons find this delay embarrassing or comic. What can be more erotic than a woman lying still as you undo buttons that she fastened before coming to see you? It is a stimulating idea and I needed to keep it fully in mind as I turned my attention to the unconscionable number of buttons on her shirt. I know that some couples break off at this stage to undress themselves but this seems too mechanical and anyway the fetishist must remain true to his fetish. I unfastened the last button and pulled the shirt apart, revealing an ornate black bra. And she'd never seen *Psycho.*

I kissed her on her lips, her prominent chin, her neck and then between her breasts. I was surprised to see a group of three or four sturdy hairs sprouting above her breastbone, which was more than she would see when I took my shirt off. It was a hot evening and her skin felt clammy to my lips. Perhaps she was nervous. I didn't know whether I was or not. I reached inside her shirt and behind her back for the clasp of her bra. I ran my finger along and tugged but there didn't seem to be one. She whispered, a nice touch, she was trying to be kind:

'It's not there. Look.' She sat up and unfastened the bra in front, at the cleavage.

I looked. Breasts are such wonderful objects. How can any woman be unhappy who has them, or has one of them, or has the memory of having had them? What an enviable thing it is to be a woman, especially a lesbian.

This is the moment when I start to consider that I'm seeing something that hardly anyone else has seen, or at least there must be close friends and colleagues who haven't seen what I'm seeing. On the other hand this is an extremely limited form of triumph since it is a privilege shared with a substantial number of strangers, including people who happened to occupy the same beach, doctors, nurses, shop assistants and so on.

Susan's breasts were large, even for her large body, and the nipples were sizeable too, dark brown and erect. She glanced down at them herself with a smile as if she were seeing them through my eyes. I touched one with my tongue and she was polite enough to gasp. Three weeks ago I hadn't even met this woman and now I was kissing her breasts.

Now things were about to get complicated once more. Jeans don't lend themselves to swift removal. They are not an article of clothing you can insinuate off with the owner barely noticing. Flares had been before my time and they may have been easier but for the sort of jeans Susan was wearing, what was really required to get them off her was two strong men and a shoehorn. Furthermore, a reconnaissance mission had reported back that she was wearing the sort of long boots that are attractive to the passive onlooker but have a lace the length of a football field wound through and round about two hundred hooks and eyes.

I began on her boots while she leant forward and worked her way down my shirt. I reached behind and tugged off my trainers along with the socks. Her boots came away with some sharp dragging. Now for her jeans. The trick, I could anticipate, was to pull the jeans off while leaving her knickers undisturbed. Pulling jeans and knickers off together was a casual intimacy reserved only for couples of long standing. I pushed myself between her legs and unfastened the fly buttons. Then grasping the waistband, with my knuckles hard against the bones of her pelvis, I gave an exploratory pull. She lifted herself co-operatively off the sofa. As I pulled the jeans down over her buttocks and down her large white shiny thighs, I wondered what it must be like to seduce a woman against her will, a pitched battle through a series of obstacles. Then I grabbed them at the ankles and whipped them over her feet and off in an undignified final flourish.

'You look wonderful,' I said. Not everyone would have agreed with this, as I could see even at the time. By the standards that obtained in the West she was unquestionably overweight. And although her hips were not fat exactly, they were of a round shape and seemed to belong to someone else, like a figure in one of those children's books with flaps that allow the reader to give a body Granny's feet, the grocer's torso and the cat's head. Was this perception, which seemed tender at the time, the first of those which I later co-opted and constructed into a rickety structure that didn't look like anything recognizable but which I was to call Love? Until later, when I rechristened it Untitled.

I was not appraising her body from any superior standpoint. After all, mine was still to come, an oddity which, unless she had accumulated her sexual experience among sumo wrestlers, was probably something the like of which she had never seen.

'Bed-time,' she said.

VI

SUSAN WAS BY this point wearing knickers, spectacles and nothing else. I had only removed my shoes and socks, though my shirt had been unbuttoned. I took her by her labourer's hands and pulled her up from the sofa. As she walked in front of me in that awkward transition to the bed, I touched her between her broad shoulders and ran my finger down the jointed snake of her spine. We used to do that to each other at school to induce a rippling shiver in the recipient. Susan sat down on the bed and I eased her down sideways so that she was lying on her back, as if she were about to recount her dreams to Dr Weaver. She smiled up at me. Was this an expression of reassurance? Of amused contempt? Of puzzlement?

The sequence of events had to be precise, there was little margin for error. It was too late to switch off the light in the main room, but if I left the light off in the recess then the atmosphere was less like that of a laboratory. I pointed my arms straight down behind me at the floor, like a swimmer preparing to dive off his block, and my shirt slipped down off me. I kissed her lightly on the lips once more. Now the spectacles really were in the way. I pulled them off, though because I forgot to tip them forward they caught awkwardly on her ears before coming free and being tossed on to the carpet. I closed her eyes with the fingers of my right hand, the way doctors do to the dead in films just before they look up and shake their head solemnly. Then, in fast motion, off with the trousers. A moment of frenzied silent struggle. There.

With the complex teamwork of hands and lips I worked my way down from her face to her breasts which, now she was lying on her back, looked smaller but still not small. Her hands moved on to my hair, but I wasn't having any of that. I needed all the concentration I could muster. I pushed her elbows back level with her ears, until she looked pleasingly like a Renaissance painting of a saint about to be subjected to an agonizing and deeply erotic form of martyrdom.

My face slid over the fleshy waves of her tummy and she stirred and gasped. Her body knew what was coming, or at least it thought it did. From an altitude of about an inch I was staring straight through the filigree work of whatever her knickers were made of at the outline of her copious dark brown pubic hair. I gave a few provisional gentle nips at the material with my teeth, then neatly and quickly hooked my index fingers into the knickers and whipped them down her legs and off, then without a pause manoeuvred myself over her left leg. My own feet were now on the carpet at the end of the bed and my head, whose hair I had washed this afternoon, whose stubble I had allowed to grow to the rightish sort of length since the day before yesterday, was positioned between her knees. With my left hand I seized the folded duvet and pulled it off the bed on to the floor behind me. I then placed each hand on a thigh, and opened them like the points of a soft, baggy compass from an angle of about forty degrees to a bold unambiguous ninety.

My hands on the inside of her thighs were trembling slightly now. Not so much a loss of nerve as a due sense of occasion. This was another stage of reflection. I remember the first time I ever faced this prospect in real life. My first thought was not, how beautiful, or how erotic, but the perception, vivid as a car crash, that real sex isn't like the movies, the beautifully lit golden brown skin viewed from a discreet angle, the fragmented editing, the soft music. No. It's low budget, badly lit, single take, hard-core pornography, and with smells and stickiness as well. More specifically relevant to the current engagement, we were now getting to a manageable number of people who had seen this sight. Parents had seen it in an earlier version, hairless and half formed when changing nappies, dressing and undressing, but that scarcely counted. And a few oblivious, amnesiac doctors and gynaecologists would have seen it in its adult state. But not one of even her very closest friends—people who had known her since nursery school, who had been on holiday with her, shared flats with her, people with whom she had cried, girls who had nursed her through breakdowns and witnessed her triumphs—had seen what I was seeing after a few meetings over less than a month. They had known her before me and would know her afterwards when I would be no more than a fading stain on her memory, but I had already seen something that they could only imagine, and perhaps secretly fantasize about.

And then there were other people who really had seen it. How many were there? A bridge four? A rowing eight? A team for soccer, rugby league or rugby union? An American football squad, the offense and the defense running out in ranks on to the trembling turf with the weight of their steroid-boosted bodies? Could they fit into a telephone box, the back seat of a car, a station wagon, a minibus, a double decker, a small lecture theatre, a minor rock venue? What would they all look like gathered together in one room, if they all showed up to the reunion party? At this moment those who were still alive were somewhere doing something else, eating, sleeping, sitting in front of computer terminals; producing television programmes, writing novels, accepting awards for bravery, humanitarianism or major creative achievements; commanding military vehicles on dangerous manoeuvres, climbing mountains, leading expeditions, cutting down trees; banging circus tent pegs into the ground, tuning up electric guitars for the evening's show, toting hods of bricks on their shoulders, descending into dark water-filled potholes, fucking someone else, but as they did so comparing it with when they had fucked—what was she called? that overweight one—and feeling a tiny memorial glow of possessive pride.

I kissed and bit the inside of Susan's right leg and then moved up. Some extra stimulation was required but not for her, not from her vertical, glistening smile. I slid my left hand under her buttocks, lifted her very slightly and drew my tongue up one of her labia—is that a labium?—and then the other. My right hand was resting on her tummy and I moved it down into her pubic hair, gripped the flesh and pulled it lightly in the direction of her face. There it was, her little glistening clitoris, peeking out. It may be that there are even members of the football team, the Fuck Society, who haven't seen that, there may even be enough who haven't seen it to form a subsidiary society of their own, to rent a little charabanc. I pushed my tongue as far as it would go into her cunt and brought it up and on to her clitoris, using the tip to deliver an experimental prod:

'Ow, no, no.' Susan's whole body twisted, trying to escape, banging my nose against a surprising bone.

This was 'no' meaning 'no', so with my eyes watering I moved my tongue into orbit and then regained entry into the slime.

A hundred years ago I would have been arrested for

writing this, though even then I, in my current state, the state in which I am attempting to re-imagine this episode, might have been excused prosecution; deportation would have been a likely alternative.

I knew, but had never understood, that there were men repelled by cunts, who didn't want to touch the horrid things, as if they were reptiles or insects. Perhaps it was the sliminess. A gay man once told me that he disliked honey because it was so intensely female. I assumed that he didn't mean the hard kind, which you have to dig your knife into and is more likely to inspire thoughts of earwax than anything else. He must have meant the lovely runny kind that drips down your knife uncontrollably. But it can't be just that. *Vagina dentata*, a cunt with teeth, a common fear, apparently, but a curious one, since there already is a female orifice with teeth. That's the one to be afraid of, the one that can insult you, humiliate you, reject you, say no. That one is enough. There's no need to find another monster to be afraid of.

Foreplay was becoming procrastination. Susan stroked my ears and my hair, then took hold of me and pulled me firmly and irrevocably up the bed until our faces were level. She looked bleary and drugged. I smiled a glistening smile at her, the flesh around my lips sticky and stinging, like a child raising its face from an unmanageably overripe mango. I had a sense of impending failure. I was going out on stage and I sensed that the lines were not there in my mind to be delivered. Susan raised herself on her right elbow and ran her finger down my chest. There was nothing to be done, my cue had arrived and the play couldn't continue without me.

'This is the point where the hero of the worst novel I've ever read says, "Have you a contraceptive?"'

She nodded.

'I'm on the pill,' she whispered.

I was inches away from the edge of the precipice but I still had time for a moment of icy anger to chill my cheeks. She didn't have a boyfriend, she'd told me, and she could hardly have gone on the pill in anticipation of this evening's grapplings. So there she was, chemically fooling her own body that it was pregnant just as a way of securing a general availability to anyone she might come across. That dark stab was something to be stored away for later. I now faced a more urgent problem. I was like a conjuror reaching into his top hat in the sure knowledge that his rabbit was AWOL. Giving me a parodically lascivious wrinkle of the nose—God, she was lovely—Susan pulled down my boxer shorts—this was 1988—and stared down at the disaster area. After all that thought and imagination.

At my school we never had sex education, and as a result there are still some pretty basic matters with which I'm not precisely *au fait*, and I never quite met the right person in the right circumstances to explain them to me. Still, what my school did provide was a biology teacher whose face went red as he pointed to a chart of three enlarged cross-sections, one dormant and one erect, both of which were bafflingly different from what all but a few of us twelve-year-olds had down our unbulging grey flannels, and a third one which seemed to make no sense at all. He told us, not entirely accurately, that the man experiences a feeling of pleasure during the act of sexual intercourse. For reasons of his own he also provided a few titbits of sexual information. The only one I remember is the ability, he claimed, of specially trained Japanese samurai warriors to retract their testicles into their body in order to protect them during combat. Useful as this might have been in a number of situations in my earlier life, I had never managed it. However, this time, contrary to my own conscious will, I had apparently achieved a further stage of enlightenment by retracting my cock substantially instead. At least that seemed to be the only plausible explanation for what had happened. It's not just that it was non-tumescent, it had scarcely shown up for duty at all. At every hint of contact it shrank further like a mole desperately attempting to retreat into a hole that was too small for it.

'Oh, dear,' said Susan, before conscience struck. 'It doesn't matter, you know.'

'It only looks so small because I'm very fat. That is actually an erection.'

'You're not with the rugby team now, my darling. You don't need to pretend. Just lie back.'

My darling. Women can be nice. Susan then massaged, stroked and bit me, before moving with an ominous sense of purpose to my groin. She caressed my cock, squeezed it as if she were milking it, licked and sucked it, all to no effect at all. Quite the reverse. An unimaginable fantasy and horribly unenjoyable. Then she hugged me, I said it was nothing to do with her, and we passed smoothly enough from the foreplay to the afterplay. She asked me if it had ever happened before. If it had ever not happened before, that is, she corrected herself charmingly. I wondered whether to say yes and make myself feel bad, or no and make her feel bad. I changed the subject (it had, of course) and we lay and talked, about people we knew and fatness and its novelties. She'd always thought *she* was fat, she said, nuzzling into one of my comfy folds. We talked about sex in general and then, guardedly, a little more specifically, and I lied judiciously.

For a physical catastrophe, the evening was a relative success. It was the Blitz spirit: people who had lost almost everything drawn together in mutual support. It was all fine, of course. A few days later, when I was not so aroused and fascinated by the sight of Susan's body as to feel a responsibility to do something in response, when it had become part of my furniture, something I could ignore or toy with, something I was used to seeing get up and waddle around to get the papers or disappear into the bathroom, then a highly abbreviated version of the above scene took place, at the end of which I presented her with an erect cock, like a bouquet.

VII

AFTER A FEW weeks we discovered that we had become a couple. We started to spend the night together more frequently than apart. We would recount to each other what we had done during the day. We would both attend a social occasion to which only one of us had been invited. In practice this meant that I accompanied her, since she had many friends and I didn't. Soon we were invited together. Postcards would arrive through either of our postboxes addressed to us both. We were Susan and Greg, and a little later we were even Greg and Susan occasionally. It was manifest to anyone that she had saved me from pariahdom, but a few of Susan's friends did me the honour of claiming, in whispered confidence, that I'd been good to her, rescued her from something, helped her.

There was no narrative thread in the destruction of our relationship, just as there is no narrative in the decay of an abandoned house. Windows break, the timbers rot, plaster cracks and falls off the wall, the brickwork crumbles, tiles are dislodged, but it all happens concurrently. Flaws that were part of the building's ramshackle charm suddenly start letting the rain in and making it uninhabitable. One day the house falls down. Or perhaps it gradually erodes to a degree where, in the eyes of a visitor, it is no longer recognizable as a house at all. But the story of the decline is of no interest to the owner or a potential buyer. He wants the damage itemized in a surveyor's report.

In fact, looking back, I can see very little narrative progression, just a process of attrition, except it wasn't her at all, it was me, drifting on a slope that was barely perceptible but whose prevailing tendency was always downwards. I never saw change occurring but I had occasional realizations that changes had occurred. After a few months Susan had, like an incoming tide filling inlets and subterranean caves, occupied my room. There was her toothbrush and a clutter of bottles for the bathroom, though they could never actually be kept there, in case they were taken in lieu of rent, or vomited on. There were the paperback novels she had read—distinguishable because they splayed open like abandoned concertinas—dotted on my shelf. Her research notes, written in a distinctively flamboyant, looping script, were scattered across the desk among my own papers. There was a jacket and a shirt left in the wardrobe, and a pair of jeans the same colour as my own. Sometimes on confused mornings I would pull her pair tight over my knees and flail helplessly like a beached mermaid. Her life was held together by a network of small objects and two jade-like green bowls on my mantelpiece were full of spare earrings, hairclips, tweezers and other less familiar instruments and adornments. More and more often, if she bought some object of the kind that I would never consider buying, like a candlestick, a vase, a stand for newspapers (that instantly became clogged and useless), it would end up in my room. She seemed to have penetrated all the cavities of my life and then one day I saw that the tide had receded. With no announcement, everything had gone, even her toothbrush from the glass. Where there was any object on which I might have a claim—the mug emblazoned with the name of a nuclear power station we had visited together—it remained. But everything else had been removed, with nothing to mark its passing except gaps on the bookshelf and circular clean shapes in the dust. The dust that she would remove, if not often, then at least more often than I would. When had she done it, all at once or in painstakingly planned steps? By this time our communication was intermittent and painful, and the question evoked in me nothing but a dull gnawing fear of what answer it might elicit from her.

We were at our best in the first days when I took her lightly. I used to love the cheerfully self-deprecating way she spoke of her earlier life, of calamities, failures, social humiliations, absurd characters, hopeless boyfriends she had got mixed up with. For the first time in my life I had met someone with whom I could at least pretend to talk about sex in an adult and casual and disinterested way. Best of all in the early days was when she was being nice to me to make up for things, and when she wasn't bothered about the impression she was making on me, though sometimes even that could be a bit of a strain. I don't know what the occasion was, or the context, but we were once a bit drunk and talking about things in the past and she said quite casually, and I remember every word of this:

'You know those times when you're young and you just fuck people out of curiosity almost?'

I wondered what a normal person ought to say in order to convey the impression that this was a conversation like any other. Something like 'I certainly do,' or perhaps just a slight laugh suggesting just how many, how absurdly many, of those times there had been and how one really just had to laugh about it now. I've not gone into detail about my past life—I don't want to get into that here—but one thing I remember from one awful brief encounter, in fact virtually the only thing I remember, was my companion saying, with what sounded to me like gloomy resignation, that 'Soon we'll all have fucked each other.' 'You can include me out of your calculations,' I should have said and didn't, but I did manage a sophisticated grunt, and it did make me feel to some extent that we were both people of the world.

But to Susan I didn't manage anything so smooth. I responded with another question:

'No, but do you know those times when you're very curious but you still don't fuck anyone at all?'

This derailed the conversation, wherever it was going, but Susan thought it was funny. I felt like a detective in a whodunnit. When all the suspects were called together in the library and I addressed them, I would begin:

'That, Susan, was your first mistake, the moment when you first gave yourself away.'

The suave veneer was not always so resolutely maintained. She used to be—used to be with me—a cruel, enchanting mimic. Traumas were retold as farces, obnoxious brutes became comic turns. Then one day a story didn't seem funny any more. With a sick feeling I asked:

'But did you let him fuck you?'

'What's that got to do with it?'

'Why can't you tell me? Did he fuck you?'

The funny routine was over. She was no longer smiling, but numbed and deliberate.

'Yes, he did.'

I realized that I must be in love with Susan. Why else would I care so much about her? I no longer saw her as a picaresque comic hero, passing through amusing adventures untouched and unstained. I could think of nothing else except the grinning simpleton she was imitating, with the wonderful monotonous voice and his terribly funny witterings on about 'lifestyles'—or was it 'lifeplans'? And yet at the end of that evening during which he had been so ludicrous, and from which Susan had stored up so much hilariously funny material, the two of them had taken their clothes off and seen each other naked and then she had let him fuck her, let him ejaculate into her cunt. Perhaps she had sucked his prick as well, the way she had sucked mine, or what there was of mine, on our first evening together. I could feel my heart like a ball, no not like a ball, like a knitting needle jabbing against the inside of my chest.

'But why, if he was such a fuckhead? Why'd you let him do it to you?'

There was a long pause.

'He was . . . He was . . . ' I'd never seen her stammer like this. It was an achievement of a kind. 'I couldn't be bothered not to. I felt shitty about it afterwards. Does that make you feel better?'

It didn't, not at all. But it stimulated my curiosity. She had felt degraded, and it made me love her sickeningly. Some time later, perhaps one of those times when we still got lightheartedly drunk, we started playing some sort of game of truth or dare, just the two of us. She asked me what my most embarrassing moment was and I lied about something not too bad which was meant, paradoxically, to show me in a favourable light, and then it was my turn to ask her a question. My ears were ringing and I gulped the first word and had to begin again:

'Truth. Tell me the name of every person you've ever slept with.'

I've already mentioned Susan's colourful cheeks which gave her, quite misleadingly, an appearance of outdoor healthiness, as if she had just scampered in from the meadow. But her face now took on an intense crimson that was entirely new. She looked down at the floor as if, for the first time, she was embarrassed to be in my presence. I wondered if she was totting up the numbers. Did she consider providing the list as a means of ending this painful subject once and for all, putting it behind us, setting our relationship on a basis of mature honesty? Once I knew the worst, I could put it aside, forgive her; there would be nothing left to fantasize about, and I could relax again. The line of her jaw flexed and she raised her big coffee-brown eyes to me.

'Fuck you,' she said.

I'd gone red as well by this time. I attempted a long, excessive, rambling apology, explaining that it was really all my fault, and that of course I didn't care how many people she'd slept with, and it was none of my business what she did before we met, and did she think I thought she should just remain a virgin, and if she had done that she wouldn't have been the girl that attracted me the way she had done, the girl who said that she would like a fur coat, who would like the sensual pleasure that a fur coat would bring. What I liked about her was the idea of her as a cat, wriggling and purring and being stroked, it was just that sometimes I was pained by the idea of her doing it with anyone apart from me, but that was entirely my fault and my problem, something she had no responsibility for at all. It was part of the way I loved her, a retrospective possessiveness, a wish that every part of her life should be mine, but that wasn't to justify it in the least, it was something I didn't just have to deal with but to cut out of my life. We had a really good discussion about it that went on for hours, and that night we made love and it was better than it had ever been, in a way. I didn't just say all this; I believed it. From then on I never questioned her about her past life at all, and I didn't sulk when old boyfriends, old lovers, old flings, old fucks, were mentioned by someone else casually in conversation, but just talked about them normally as if they were natural topics of conversation. I think we sorted it out to an extent, but she was hardly ever so funny in the same way again. She stopped referring to her past. I don't think it was a conscious decision on her part, it just never seemed to come up in the way it once had.

I've struggled over and over with this section of my story. The reader will clearly be able to see the insertions, the crossings out, contradictions, alterations of emphasis that testify to changes of mind. Looking through my description of our relationship, I wonder whether it isn't still misleading. This is not the way the story, such as it was, seemed at the time. When our relationship finished, I plundered my memory for the conflicts and miseries that were lying there, stinging and throbbing, and tried to join them together in such a way that they would cohere, in the manner that our life as a couple ultimately and unquestionably did. That it began is a fact and that we parted is a fact, but I can't speak with much conviction of anything that happened in between. My jaundiced, self-inculpating sift through that baffling couple of years ignores all the happy occasions. They are somehow rendered inapplicable or false by the unhappy ending. I could describe all the things that I never would have done on my own, a picnic, for example—wine, ants, cheese and bread, open-air copulation. We went abroad once, to Amsterdam; we didn't find anywhere to stay and gawped at people dealing dope in a hippyish café. We once played a real dare game, I mean an enjoyable one, where each of us had to phone up somebody we knew and pretend to be someone else. I rang up some poor girl at work pretending to be the tracing department of a VD clinic. I loved Susan for finding something so cruel so funny.

In theory the nicest thing she ever did was to buy me a copy of *Henry IV Part Two* and inside she wrote: 'Banish plump Greg and banish all the world.' That was overwhelmingly nice at the time except that it happened somehow too late in the relationship. What would at one time have been impulsive and emotional by then seemed calculated and self-conscious. It was a cute gesture which was like an imitation of what a person in love would do, by someone who was no longer in love and had lost the knack. Moreover, as I was to discover, it was the gesture of someone who was about to have no problem at all in banishing plump Greg without the fear that the world would be affected in any way. And if one is going to be literary and pedantic instead of having real emotions, then one might as well point out that the quotation is actually from Part One, not Part Two, unless I've misunderstood the point of the reference.

Then there was sex in its more direct sense which by the end, admittedly, was a pitiful, virtually masturbatory affair. I was almost embarrassed, lying sticky and panting afterwards, by the presence of someone else in the bed, even if all I could see was her large silent back. My version of the disastrous first night sounds unpropitious, but I've missed out the successes in between. There were the early months when we couldn't keep our hands off each other, where it was as if I didn't have to do anything to make her want me. We'd fuck in the morning and at night, in the bathroom at parties, in the stacks of the London Library, on a stone bridge on Hampstead Heath one morning in early autumn with me standing nervously behind her while she just laughed and leant over the parapet looking at the swans swimming below. I know this reads like the script for a bad film montage, but I'm concerned that I'm doing a better job of describing why Susan got sick of me than why she was actually attracted to me in the first place.

Nor do I want to make it sound as if it were just me tormenting a blameless woman. She had faults, and irritating qualities. She could be moody and selfish. Her capriciousness was part of her charm but it could also be a bore, on the rare occasions when I had work to do or people to see. I could quote examples, there are plenty, but it would sound petty to cite them here, one by one. The problem with describing the little daily offences that cause irritation is that in the telling they suddenly stop seeming serious enough to have been worth remembering.

But I'm sorry, this is all wrong. I'm setting out to do precisely what I wanted to avoid, which is to contest an argument that is finished and was never a matter of rational debate anyway. I'm searching for causes that I can attach to an incontrovertible effect, but in the end it was more like an incontrovertible mood. What I feel nostalgic for is the sense of effortless power. At my first, accidental lunch with Susan I felt what it was to be endlessly amusing and interesting, though the curse is that I didn't feel it at the time. I valued myself, when what I should have been doing was valuing her attention and the effect it had on my conversational tropes, which in reality were no different from what they had been in their ineffective past and were to be again in their ineffective future. And on our first night together my bathetic impotence was a triumph because it showed that mere success was an irrelevance.

I spent one of our evenings apart, of which there were by this stage an increasing number, working all this out. It was a cruel paradox. Susan loved the Greg who didn't care deeply for her, thereby permitting her to treat her own life lightly. Greg was made to love Susan by the adoring response she gave to the aforementioned pre-lover version of Greg. The fact of loving Susan meant he could no longer collude in Susan's attempts at belittling herself. Susan now hated Greg because he had become a colluder in her self-hatred, the very problem that she thought Greg would help her solve. I tried to explain this to Susan on the phone very late one night, but she was crying and she hung up. This may not have been such a bad thing because, had she grasped the argument, she might have pointed out its basic flaw, which is that according to its logic, I ought to have ceased loving her once she cut off the flow of approbation which made my own life seem a success, whereas I continued to be addicted to her. I found it physically harrowing to be apart from her, even when I knew that our proximity resulted in equally harrowing silences and squabbles.

Alternatively the whole syllogism could have been based on error. It could be argued that my cruelty about her past cannot be dignified by the claim that I was in some way taking her seriously. It might also be suggested that her own evasive attitude to the failings of her past life was itself an obstacle. Either of our disabilities could have destroyed the relationship on its own, but together they ensured it stood no chance at all.

While I was wrestling with these problems, I received a letter.

VIII

THE TEXT OF Susan's Dear Greg letter does not survive, but it was pretty much the standard rejection. The editor thanks you for your contribution but regrets he is unable to use it. Thank you for your manuscript, which, unfortunately, we are not able to consider for publication. Dear Sir or Madam, I am afraid that due to the present economic climate, we do not see ourselves being able to renew your contract at the end of this year. May I take this opportunity to wish you a happy Christmas and best wishes for the future. Dear Mr Weaver, I am sorry for the delay in replying to you but we were overwhelmed with applications for the post for which you applied. We have now compiled a list of applicants we wish to interview, and I regret to say that your name is not on it. Dear Mr Weaver, I am afraid the post has already been filled. However, we will keep your letter on file in case any suitable vacancy should arise. Dear Greg, I think we ought to stop seeing each other. Then blah blah blah blah for about a page and then there was a genuine surprise about halfway down on the other side of the single sheet of lilac-coloured paper. I quote from memory but the words are accurate: 'I feel I ought to tell you before you hear it from anyone else that I am seeing someone else. Please believe me that this has nothing to do with what went wrong. I think for a bit it would be better if we didn't see each other at all or have any contact at all. I'm sure we can be friends again one day. I feel damaged by this too.' And then her signing off in that big, cartoonish signature, though on this particular letter I recall it was reduced slightly in thoughtful acknowledgement of the sombreness of the occasion.

I read the letter once and then folded it, returned it to its envelope and never opened it again. I wondered what other documents or objects connected with her survived in my room. I rummaged through the capacious drawer into which unsorted bric-à-brac generally found its way. I found five cards, two birthday cards, one Valentine's card, a card from when she had gone to stay with her father in Yorkshire and a little squib she had once sent on impulse when we happened to spend a couple of days apart. I began to make a small pile to which I added a squiggly little hairband from the mantelpiece. I scrutinized the shelves and saw a black-spined Penguin Classic with the characteristic white stress marks of a book that had not just been read but turned inside out and scraped clean like a fig. I looked at the inside cover: S. Gower 2.2.88. I added it to the pile. I looked under the bed and found one pink sock, the wrapper from a Tampax packet and a loop of dental floss. On a shelf I found the cracked top of some kind of make-up container and a hairpin. Then finally under some papers was a folder, neatly marked in her strangely rounded block capitals: FROM REALISM TO FABLE. I opened it. It was empty.

It was a poor unevocative haul, hardly enough to do anything to. I decided that I must have things of my own I didn't need. I climbed on my chair and pulled down a large cardboard box from behind a canvas bag on top of the wardrobe. It was speckled grey with dust but I could recognize a university essay at the top of a pile, the lower strata of which contained writings from grammar school, and finally, at the primeval level, finger paintings of half-imagined, half-remembered animals, stiff-legged under garish yellow suns. The box was not even half full and there was plenty of space on top for Susan's remnants. I picked the box up and walked like a popcorn salesman in a cinema down the stairs and out into the back garden to which I had no right of access. But it was a bit early in the morning for Vera, and besides, I would be right at the end where she wouldn't notice. The whole garden looked like wasteground but I found a particularly desolate patch next to the bulging wall. The box looked sadly small and insignificant.

'The pyre needs to be bigger,' I said aloud.

I returned to my room. I didn't take any of the furniture,

anything mechanical or any of the books or records, which I reckoned wouldn't burn, but everything else was transported to the back of the garden in a series of puffing trips up and down the stairs. Scrapbooks, old articles, paid and unpaid bills, old cheque books, my new cheque book, my paying-in book, hundreds of letters received, my two old invitations, bundles of old photographs, a small painted wooden horse. I emptied the contents of my filing cabinet into a Safeway shopping bag. I paused for a moment at a file labelled Documents. It contained my passport, my national insurance card, an envelope of premium bonds given to me by my grandfather when I was born, a building society book. These didn't matter. I was a person, I didn't need pieces of paper to tell me who I was and give me status. A surviving vestige of prudence compelled me to put the passport into my trouser pocket. On the last trip I took my clothes, quite a small sad pile really, all except the ones I was wearing. At the last moment I remembered my wallet. I extracted the contents: a credit card, a Eurocheque card which had never been used, a card for the machine in the wall of my building society, the number for which I had never known, an expired card to give me cheap entry to sporting facilities in the borough, a driving licence, a receipt for typing paper, a library card, a donor card permitting my kidneys, corneas, heart, lungs, liver and pancreas to be used after my death, two business cards, a yellowed newspaper clipping reviewing a round-up of world music albums, three Russian stamps, Susan's RAC membership card, a phonecard, Susan's membership of the National Trust, a piece of paper bearing a phone number attached to a name whose significance I could no longer remember, a receipt from Thomas Cook for changing guilders into sterling, a handwritten recipe for coffee ice cream, one British Rail credit card sales voucher, one ten-pound note and two five-pound notes. Everything, apart from the cash, was tipped on to the heap.

I returned to the house and searched the washroom inside the door for some sort of inflammable liquid. Why do 'flammable' and 'inflammable' mean the same thing? I opened a cupboard. White spirit. Highly flammable. Good. And matches as well. I sprinkled the heady liquid over the now substantial pile and then just emptied it into the middle, tossing the bottle on as well. As I applied the match there was a low thud and then a rush of flame and crackling, and almost immediately my life began to glow orange. It felt marvellously warm against my face and hands in the chill spring morning. Everything had gone. Almost everything. I took the passport out of my pocket. I saw that the corner had been cut off. It was an old one. I opened it and looked at the glassy-eyed round-faced eighteen-year-old. Fatboy, they used to call me, a nickname I had never much minded, and even less after I read *The Pickwick Papers.* The fat boy who likes to make your flesh creep. I thought of the only time I could remember making an instantaneous and funny riposte. Susan had quoted to me Cyril Connolly's saying that inside every fat man is a thin man trying to get out. And I said, 'I don't know about that. With me it's more a case of a fat man who has spent his life trying to get into lots of thin women.' I thought that was so clever it was almost like being the leading character in a film or play, in fact as I said it I felt at the same time that it seemed a bit too clever, as if it had been rehearsed and saved up. But Susan was still at that time a good audience. She laughed and laughed. If the positions had been reversed, I would probably have refused sullenly to laugh because of the reference to previous sexual activity, even when couched in the form of sexual non-activity, but Susan was always very good about things like that, not that, of course, there was much to be good about.

As the fire continued to roar I sat on the low mossy wall, over which boys would clamber after lost balls or with the intention of burglary, and looked through heat and smoke at the house. After a minute or two a white-haired, red-faced apparition emerged and glided towards me, rippling through the air currents above the blaze.

'What a nice thing,' said Vera. 'A winter fire.'

'It's spring,' I said. 'Can't you see? Everything's growing and changing.'

IX

SUSAN WAS NO longer living at her flat. But it only took a relatively small number of cleverly ulterior-motivated phone calls to discover where she was. She had moved in with her new man. He was called Tony, he was a doctor, he was reputed to be nice, and he lived over there in that house, the little white one. When she met me, Susan had got into the wrong lift, though she was too polite to say so straight away. She had meant to go up and found herself going down. The mistake had finally been corrected and she was clearly going in the right direction now. If I may shift from vertical metaphor to horizontal reality, fifteen stops and about an hour and a half on the Northern Line had brought me to a dinky little toytown terrace in Camden Town with houses all joined together and painted different pastel colours: pink, blue, yellow, cream, white-ish. It was, I had to admit, a very, very nice piece of property. If, for purposes of comparison, the scrap value of my room and its contents was roughly nothing, then this house here, about two bedrooms, fitted carpets, gas CH, little garden behind, I would imagine—and this was now 1989—must have been worth about 190,000 pounds, any day of the week. I felt a woozy happiness on Susan's behalf. Good old Susan. She was all right now.

I had not used the time between the pyromaniac destruction of effects that morning and this exterior surveillance particularly productively, but I had bought a bottle of vodka with a Russian name manufactured in Britain under licence to an American company. And I had bought a carton of orange juice, 'A blend of pure Orange Juice from more than one country of origin.' What an effort to get those oranges from different countries, from Spain, Morocco, Israel, South Africa, perhaps somewhere else which made them particularly cheaply, and to fit them into that small packet. The result was not exactly orange juice, but it was better than orange juice. It was a tribute to orange juice. I had then mixed the contents, fifty-fifty, in an opaque plastic bottle that was designed for taking on picnics, camping expeditions, up mountains, across snowy wastes where it might freeze. Or not, if it were filled with my vodka concoction. Which my bottle no longer was. It was now half filled and stowed in the pocket of my baggy surviving coat.

I used to suffer from an unusual, indeed so far as I know unique, form of claustrophobia. Closed spaces didn't disturb me in the least. Quite the contrary. When I was a child I used to have a fantasy of living my life alone in a lavishly equipped, snug-fit midget submarine, drifting slowly round the world peering at whales and sharks. My claustrophobia took the form of an occasional fear of being trapped within my own body. For the most part I loved my body, a fleshy slab of a size which made me feel sometimes that I'd colonized it, like the East India Company perched on the edge of the subcontinent. One day it would wake up and realize that it could get by without me. Just sometimes, though, I would feel a prickle of frustration just like the occasional shiver of fear you get when you think, really think, about the fact that you will one day sense correctly that you are a few moments away from dying and vanishing for ever, unless, that is, you die in your sleep or are knocked over by a bus from behind and killed instantly. But the idea of insensibility for eternity seemed more of a comfort than anything else. What distressed me was the bit before that, the prospect of being trapped for all my earthly existence in this puffing, smelly, baggy, inefficient machine. The vodka was good for that. I could feel my frame slowly breaking up like a cloud, becoming indistinct like water in water. For a time the barriers between me and everything else didn't seem absolute.

I had no idea why I had come to look at Susan's house. Suddenly I felt affectionate towards her. Poor lonely sad woman. I hoped she would have a happy life. Perhaps I should knock at the door just to wish her a happy life.

It was time to go. I walked to the main road and turned right, in the direction of the tube station. A couple of people asked me for money but then saw that I was as drunk and hopeless and homeless as they were. I needed to get away; I needed to walk down a country lane lined with poplars and beech trees, listening to the ripple of running water. As if it were granted by Providence I found myself passing on the right a gate leading down to the canal. That would do. I climbed up and wondered how I would get down. As it happened I didn't have to move at all. The ground co-operatively came up towards me and then rolled me down the steps on to the path. That was easy. My forehead felt warm and wet. I took a tissue from my pocket and mopped the wetness. I felt nothing but I knew that someone had a stinging pain. How terrible that must be.

I took a gulp of my improvised Screwdriver and turned right. The water of the canal was not running, but it was rippling, the full moon shattering and re-forming, shattering and re-forming. There were some complicated manoeuvres—I felt myself moving across a bridge, or was it two?—and then miraculously I was away from the traffic, now nothing more than the stray toot of a horn, the roar of an accelerating car. I was alone except for these numb feet below me that seemed to be carrying me along at a fascinatingly high speed. And things were being seen. The canal was being looked at, and sometimes the sky and the paved walkway flung themselves into view. One particular paving stone leant forward for a gravelly kiss, then receded and was left behind by those active feet.

The forward movement had stopped. The solid sense of a bench, and behind the bench, black against the black sky, something big. Something heard. I told the buzzing head to be quiet. Tweets and flutters. I knew. It was the great cathedral of a bird cage. All around was London Zoo. Over the other side of the canal were the dim outlines of cages and barred houses. No animals visible, all locked inside. But behind were preliminary sounds—throat clearings, scales being practised in preparation for the dawn chorus to greet the light that was gathering below the horizon from where I had just come. I was unable to move. I was unable to be moved. I saw something to my right. It was an arm. Strange. I looked to my left. It was another arm. A rational remnant in some recess of my mind knew that these belonged in a loosely proprietorial sense to my body, but I didn't feel it was mine. I had no ability or wish to do anything with it, to use it for anything. I felt no more connection with it than I felt with the birds that I heard attempting their first useless caged flaps of the day. I tried to think of my life, the husk of which was somewhere down at the other end of the Northern Line, and I felt no connection to that either. I didn't want it. Someone else could take it, if they could find any use for it.

I felt a spurt of excitement. Where did I feel it? What did I feel it with? I had escaped from my body and my life as if from an insane asylum and the one thing I knew was that I didn't want go back. I didn't want the men in white coats of consciousness to come and drag me back into that body and force me to return to that life and put its boring burned pieces back together. I made a silent prayer to any god, devil, local deity, earth spirit, that might be listening. Please, please, please. I don't expect to get away with it entirely. But give me a free transfer. If I've got to go back, then there's so much to choose from, put me back somewhere else. Put me back into one of the birds and let me fly south where it's blue and warm. Please please. I don't want a long life, I just don't want mine.

Slowly the dawn slid towards me and sleep fell.

PART TWO

THE REALM OF THE SENSES

I

I LAY CURLED around myself on the ground, a furry hillock, feigning sleep, as the predictable radio show of reality got underway. The approaching sounds of leather-soled shoes on the path. A hollow rasp as the bucket touched the gravel. The metallic throat-clearing of keys being removed from a pocket and then a sharp cough as one was inserted in the lock of the cage door, which then gave its daily whine of protest. With a spring that came easily to me now—I had tested it, leaping delightedly from bar to bar every day for a week—I flew past the clumsy snatching arms, disabled by keys and bucket, and was free.

Ungratefully abandoning my second birthplace, I looked around me. A path stretched away beyond my sight. Too dangerous. I leapt over a fence and plunged into the bushes where I felt safe. At high speed, I padded my way through on my feet and hands. Fun. I was designed for this, and at first I just enjoyed my new liberty and the untested power of my small, wiry limbs. There would be a search and my urgent priority was safety, but that I was able to achieve with an ease that was almost pitiful. Up and over cages and roofs, and then I reached a perimeter wall. Out of habit I looked for a door or at least some mechanical aid, remembered myself and simply ran up its rough brickwork, then thrillingly leapt down to a friendly projecting branch.

In a few more soft vertical steps I was at the top of the tree, invisible to any earthbound observer. I lay back in the warmth of the strengthening morning sun and began absently to pick at my fur for the fleas that were so irritating at the beginning and end of each day. I found one, held it up for inspection and then absent-mindedly chewed on it while considering what my medium-term strategy ought to be. Abstract thought had become a tiring occupation and within a few minutes I was asleep.

My wish to become a bird had not been granted. But through some higher organizing wisdom, or perhaps an extra-sensory crossed line, I had woken up on the morning after my *Walpurgisnacht* as a monkey. What kind? I don't know, since the label on the cage is designed for those outside looking in, rather than those inside looking out. I'm small, of an indeterminate brown colour and an apparently equable temperament, but beyond that there is not much that I can say. Was the metamorphosis a shock? A relief, rather. I had escaped from the world of anxieties and necessary observances into a smaller existence of smells, tastes, sounds, sights and sensory stimulations in a highly controlled environment.

Speaking of which, my initial impulse was, as old POWs used to say, to sit out the war in comfort, with the prospect of being waited on into a cosseted old age, with food, companionship and as many bars to swing on as anyone could possibly desire. But the food began to pall after my first few experiences of it and the company soon became insupportably wearisome. I refer not to the imbeciles who poked their tongues out at me and their fingers through the bars—how I longed to seize and sever one, but dared not face the consequences. I mean of course my new compatriots. Admittedly, having fleas plucked from one's inaccessible rear regions is a pleasure so intense as to outweigh almost any imposition, but the banality of animal society together with the rank zoological odours and the sheer concrete monotony of the deranged life of confinement proved swiftly to be intolerable.

When I woke from a brief dream of an earlier existence, I knew immediately what my destination must be. I had no conception of what I should do when I reached it, but I knew it was imperative. But patience was required. Without access to a library, I had no means of knowing whether I was primarily a nocturnal animal or not—I certainly still felt drowsy—but it was clear that it was only safe for me to travel at night, and even then only with the greatest caution. I could move quickly but I doubted whether I could outrun a dog in the open. Food was a more immediate challenge. I picked a leaf and chewed at it. It was disgusting, but was this squeamish atavism or was my disgust a physiological warning against an unsuitable form of diet? Better to play it safe. The sun was delightful, but how would I survive in winter? That problem could wait. I settled back and slumbered once more.

I enjoyed that evening's escapade—perhaps I was a night creature. Another change for the better. I flitted across Primrose Hill from tree to tree, wary for any stray dog or fox whose curiosity or playfulness I might stimulate. I reached a fence, squeezed through to a pavement and scampered across a road. The pavement was quick but too dangerous; the rooftops were safe, but precarious in the dark, and too slow. I compromised by making my way along fences and garden walls. The only attention I received was from a cat that I sent wailing on its way with a scratch across the nose. Through a miscalculation of my way through the *terra incognita* of north London, I found myself faced with an expanse of railway lines, a quarter of a mile without even a bush for cover. I sped silently across, faced with no peril other than the howling monster of an express train, until I reached the safety of the embankment on the far side. Then more fences, a main road and a further mile of gardens in neat rows.

Finally, shivering with cold—this was manifestly not my climate—I recognized the chocolate-box street and the unlucky number on the door. I was here. But what to do now? The three windows at the front were shut and the

Editorial: 2-3 Hanover Yard Noel Road London N1 8BE 071 704 9776
Sales and Publicity: 27 Wrights Lane London W8 5TZ 071 416 3000

Here is a review copy of

THE IMAGINARY MONKEY

by

Sean French

to be published on

25 March 1993

at

£12.99

Please ensure that no review appears before publication date.
We should appreciate a copy of your review.

Further information from

Granta Books are published in association with Penguin Books Ltd by Granta Publications Ltd
Registered in England No 164 2045 Registered office: 2-3 Hanover Yard Noel Road London N1 8BE

terrace of houses allowed no way through, but it was an easy matter for me to make my way up the façade, over the roof and down the other side, where the flap of a window was open. I squeezed through with ease and found myself in Susan and Tony's kitchen.

II

AS I TRIED to distinguish shapes in the dark room, I smelt a piercing scent of fruit—something citrus, two things, one bitter, one sweet, unripe bananas, a pear, something I couldn't recognize—reminding me that I had not eaten since the previous night. My knowledge of animal diet was scanty in the extreme, but Tarzan films and chimpanzee's tea parties had left me with the conviction that fruit was a good idea. I'd also seen a television documentary which suggested that I could eat meat, even monkey meat, but that particular ethical dilemma was unlikely to arise in the present environment. I felt my way through the darkness towards what I inferred to be the fruit bowl. My outstretched fingers touched some sharp objects, a metallic bunch of flowers, kitchen implements standing in a jar, then smiling slatted jaws, a toaster, then the cool rim of a china bowl and the welcome rubbery skin of a banana. I began to chew it without peeling it. A minute's silent munching and it was gone. Then something plasticky, star shaped. I took an exploratory bite. Quite nice. Then an orange, peel and all. Now for the larger globe. I nudged the bowl and it was snatched away by the darkness. Something was going to happen now. What was it? The bowl shattered on the kitchen floor.

I froze in terror and then scuttled forward, nails rattling on the wooden floor of the kitchen, then silent on the carpet of the front room. A rectangle of light was cast on the wall from the street outside. I could see stairs, the front door, a dining table. I retreated under it as I heard shuffling sounds from upstairs. Padded steps descended the stairs and I saw a pair of naked legs circling the table. A light blazed on and I let out a squeak and collided with a table leg. A stick poked me in the ribs, knocking me over, and I scrambled across the room emitting a raucous screech as I did so. Was there anywhere to hide? Blinded and dazed I careered into the corner by the front door.

'It's a fucking great rat.'

Darkly, high above me, I was aware of something advancing. Another voice spoke.

'No, it's not, it's a little monkey. Look, the poor thing's terrified.'

I looked up. These eyes were harder to focus. There we were together, Susan, Tony and Greg. Three trembling naked primates.

'Perhaps it's rabid.'

'Don't be soft,' said the familiar reassuring tones. 'Get it something to eat and drink.'

Tony's buttocks disappeared into the darkness of the kitchen. A light came on. An echoing voice from a distance.

'It's already had some.' He returned with some grapes and a saucer of water.

'Shall I use these to lure it outside?'

'Give them to me.'

I had to do this right. There would only be one chance. Over the next half hour I gradually became tamer and more trusting. By the time we had reached the last grape, I was eating from Susan's hand and giving sweet little squeaks.

'Shouldn't we take him somewhere? To the zoo or something?'

'My darling love, haven't you heard that the zoo is going to close down? If we take him back he'll just be shot with all the other endangered species.'

I had known all that talk about fur coats was bluster. Meanwhile Tony was thinking, standing naked in the middle of his front room. Such a short time together and standing so casually naked talking things over. He had a strong, dark body, the muscles well defined. His hairy chest descended and turned into his pubic hair. And then his long shadowy cock. I could see a vein, almost a tube running down from the base to the tip of the foreskin. Bigger than mine. Virtually bigger than *me*. Proportionately, though, proportionately it might be more of a contest.

'I hate pets. You can always tell a house with pets, fur and the smell of piss everywhere. The people who live there have lost control of their own environment. It's like a house with a baby in it, or small children. Everything's just a bit grubby.'

Susan tactfully changed the subject with a story that I'd heard before about how she'd never been allowed to have a pet because of her big brother's asthma. Once, though, she had to take the class hamster home for the weekend. She let it out to play in her room with the door closed but it escaped through a hole in the floorboards. For the whole weekend they could hear it under the floor, scratching around, giving the occasional squeak, and they spent hours trying to lure it to the hole with carrots, bits of birdseed, chocolate, slices of meat, anything they thought a hamster might like. But it never returned, exploring far and wide in the corners of the room until the noises stopped altogether. She spent the rest of her girlhood sleeping over the hamster's unmarked grave. She finished her anecdote with a question.

'Do you think he's toilet-trained?'

I tried to give a reassuringly toilet-trained-sounding squeak.

'The problem is,' said Tony, 'that a pet always seems exciting at first and then becomes a chore. Endless walks and grooming and getting food.'

'You don't have to take a monkey for walks. It'll be happy just jumping around the house.'

'Look, it's a big decision, it has to be planned. This thing just jumped through the window. It may be dangerous. Perhaps it will grow up to be a gorilla.'

'Tony, just let yourself be spontaneous. This has just happened. Embrace it.'

His resistance was crumbling.

'Don't we need an import licence or something? He may be from an endangered species.'

'Let's just try him out as a pet. If you don't like it after a couple of days, well, we'll just do what other people do and flush him down the bog and he can live with the other pets in the sewers.'

Tony came forward and squatted next to her, his big cock and balls pendulous. He smiled and kissed her forehead.

'OK, my love.'

I had been the means of bringing them closer together.

'What do we do with him now?'

'Put him in the kitchen with some fruit. I'll put some newspaper down.'

Very tenderly she put her hand under my bottom and lifted me up, holding me next to her lovely brown nipple, the newborn baby she had not yet had. Tony was walking upstairs. He stopped, leant over the banister and shouted.

'If it's going to be your surrogate baby, then you ought to give it a name.'

Susan looked me in the eyes and bit her lower lip in mischievous thought in the way I loved.

'I think I'll call him Greg.'

There was a laugh from the landing.

You fucking bitch. I could have scratched her right then, anywhere I wanted, but I didn't. It would have been too quick and easy. It wouldn't have hurt enough. I'd find a better way.

III

THERE IS A piquant pleasure in having the run of other people's homes when they are away. It is partly the glow of intimacy, partly the thrill of violation. I remember once as a small boy in my previous life—how terrible, now I think of it, that I never had the experience of clinging to a furry mother's breast, so preferable to the scoldings and withheld affections that were my human lot—I was hired for a few shillings to visit a house every day, in order to prevent squatters assuming possession while the owner was away. I have no idea precisely what I was supposed to do if I found intruders on the premises; I was only twelve years old at the time. On each five-minute visit during the two-week contract I would open a different drawer and examine its contents. Though I had vague hopes of stumbling across blackmail letters or pornography of an unimaginably obscene type, I found nothing. Yet there was nevertheless a thrill in fingering tea towels or lawyers' letters or articles of clothing, like exposing a tomb to the air for the first time in millennia.

I was soon a household pet, trusted not to piss on the carpet or scratch the postman through the letterbox, so when Tony went to work and when, after much dawdling, Susan went to the library, the house was all mine. My research was somewhat hampered by my need to have a lengthy sleep during the day. There have been one or two other changes in my observable behaviour. I cannot speak. I have a generalized memory of what the experience of speaking used to be like but the means by which words in my mind can be expressed in sounds through the controlled exhalation of air—that's gone. Unmourned. It never did me anything but harm. I realized that I could still write, and I determined that the written word would be the vehicle for what imaginative vigour remained to me. I resolved to spend my nocturnal hours recording my experiences while they still seemed of importance to me. It was none too soon. Now that my narrative has overtaken my transformation I feel that I have climbed up a ladder and then kicked it away behind me.

The mechanics of writing presented little problem. Pen and paper were easy to steal. Their concealment presented more of a challenge, but my explorations in this dwarfish dwelling soon revealed a high shelf on which stood a dusty complete edition of the Waverley novels, doubtless awaiting Tony's retirement or a long convalescence. Each night I stow my manuscripts behind these books and I have little doubt that this will be satisfactory for as long as is needed. If not, then this narrative will reach a sudden halt and your correspondent will doubtless be transported to a place of confinement where the top of his skull will be sawn off and electrodes will be inserted in his brain for the rest of his unnatural life.

Let me turn from that dismal prospect to the subject of my small kingdom, my new found land, as it was when first mine to explore. As must be clear from my initial nocturnal adventure on the premises, the front door gave straight on to the room which formed the whole of the ground floor, except for the kitchen behind, a relatively new extension to this workman's cottage. The front room contained a heavy wooden dining table, too large for its setting, a television and, against one wall, shelves holding books and compact discs. From this room stairs led up to the only other floor. My drunken exterior observation had not been entirely correct. This was what was known optimistically as a three-bedroom house. Starting from the back there was a rather sad, cold appendage (it was the inadequately insulated top floor of the extension) containing a spare bed and a trunk belonging to Susan which I could not open. Then came a rickety bathroom, which I avoided. I was by now adept at grooming myself and had developed an aversion to water beyond the few drops I drank, and I used to amuse my hosts by catching those on my tongue from the kitchen tap. Next was Tony and Susan's bedroom. Notice, I write it dispassionately without ironic comment. This small room contained a double bed, two fitted, slatted wardrobes, bookshelves and a further shelf on which Susan kept far more bottles, lotions and potions than had ever found their way to my bed-sitting room. The front room, the most elegant and the sunniest in the house, I associate with the rattling echo raised even by my pittering footsteps across the polished wooden expanse of the floor, broken only by a rough rug of some vaguely tribal origin—it stirred no blood memories in me. The furniture consisted of a roll-top desk and a filing cabinet, which I marked down for further exploration, and the table where Susan worked. There was also a sofa and a small black standard lamp, jointed like the skeleton of a pterodactyl. And that, apart from a mean exterior court-yard and an utterly inaccessible loft, was my finite universe.

IV

I HAD LIMITLESS time, or so it seemed. I still have no knowledge of the life expectancy of my race. I know that small dogs live longer in general than big dogs. Is the same true of monkeys? Indeed, is it true of dogs? Is it not the other way round? In any case, there was no pressing deadline for me to learn what I wished and work what mischief I could. My first cursory survey of my new world was of objects on exposed surfaces. Only a few minutes of observation enabled me to note that Susan had moved in with all her possessions, the few kitchen implements that she possessed incorporated in comradely fashion with those of Tony.

There was little to surprise me in the bathroom, though I noticed that Tony used an electric razor, necessary because his growth forced him to shave both in the morning and in the evening when he returned from work. In a pleasingly Holmesian sense, the most striking object was the one that wasn't there. I am puzzled now, in retrospect, by the human faculty for perceiving absence. I remember leaving places and being assailed by the sure sense of something not being there. I would move my hands, rotate my head in search of the precise sensation that I wasn't experiencing, and then I would realize that I had lost my hat or my gloves, or whatever it was.

The dog that didn't bark in Tony's bathroom was that shiny card, never quite flat, that Argus-eyed container of contraceptive pills which Susan would blind one by one until the month's ration was complete. There were just a few possible reasons for its absence. Tony was a doctor and he might well, out of love and professional disapproval, have advised her, an overweight smoker, to try another method. Not the cap, evidently, since there was no sign of that either. An IUD perhaps. Then there was a more sinister possibility altogether. Was she attempting to conceive? This might account for her maternal adoption of your author.

I was, as I soon discovered, skilful in some matters and as helpless as a baby in others. Few areas of the house, however apparently inaccessible, were beyond my nimble, grappling arms and legs. My hands and fingers possessed a skill and dexterity far beyond the mutton chop hands I had previously been encumbered with, but I was crucially lacking in strength. One evening they took me up to bed with them, placing me on the bed as clothes and underwear were casually thrown off. Susan had brought a handful of grapes with her and while Tony read a magazine she tossed them to me one by one in response to which I performed a trick of throwing myself into an incomplete reverse somersault, which they thought they had taught me. Tony tossed the magazine aside:

'Let me have a go.' He snatched the grapes away from her as she gave a mock protest. He tossed a couple in my direction but he wasn't really interested in me. He playfully began to throw them to Susan who failed disastrously to reach them, falling forwards on to him, almost crushing me. They were both laughing and then, I saw, kissing, first flirtatiously then deeply and carnivorously. For a deluded moment I wondered at their lack of shame and then recalled that I was under eighteen inches high, considered impercipient and posed no threat to anyone. Excluded from their play, I found myself by the door which was closed. I pushed my tiny nails into the gap and pulled at it with little result. I had an excuse for staying, so I turned and witnessed the incarnation of a scene that I had imagined dozens of times, abstractly and impersonally. Susan fucking someone else.

She broke free from the kiss and began to move ominously down his chest and stomach. Oh, no, don't you dare. She took Tony's semi-flaccid cock between her thumb and first two fingers and kissed its head lightly, and then smiled up at its proud owner. Then she placed much of it in her mouth and sucked it like a soft stick of rock, a soft stick of rock that said 'Who's Greg?' all the way through.

It may seem difficult to believe, particularly if the reader of this happens to be female, but I had never throughout the whole course of my human life seen an erect male penis except for my own, and that only on an intermittent and irregular basis. In this lack of experience I was typical only of a certain restricted subset of my gender. I was educated in the British state educational sector, at a single sex school, but nevertheless as stolidly and sullenly heterosexual an institution as exists in the world. At private boarding school, so far as I understand it, much of one's puberty and adolescence is spent, voluntarily or not, in the contemplation and manipulation, perhaps even the incorporation, of the erect members of one's fellow students. There, whatever the other benefits of this systematic preparation for leadership, the British boy receives a practical acquaintance with circumference and length, angle of projection and the remarkable varieties of shape, not to mention its liquid products and accompanying hair, testicles and so on, that the rest of us only receive from dry, unevocative text books. Much the same could be said of service in the lower ranks of the navy, or a prison sentence. It is scarcely necessary to add that practising male homosexuals are in a different category altogether, perhaps more directly comparable with the experiences of women.

It is difficult enough for me to speak of the common experiences of men. With women, it also depends on whom you select as typical. It is a matter of some doubt whether my grandmother—the one I knew—ever saw the erect sexual organ of my grandfather. She died when I was eleven, but I remember a frail paper-thin woman, who appeared detached as a matter of decorum from animal activities such as copulation or even the eating of food, which when called upon to perform she would do with fastidious distaste. Copulation certainly took place—my human mother inherited enough of her steely wispy wistfulness for me to be sure of that—but my grandmother would have been eminently capable of arranging for the sordid act to happen without her actually having to look at its uncouth and slimy instruments.

But to escape with relief from my grandmother's jejune sensual history, it might be estimated that the average youngish female reader of my stray pages may have seen, indeed touched, a number in the low double figures, perhaps fifteen or more, if those eager, craning cadet organs in the backs of cars, in cinemas, in upstairs rooms at parties, out in providential patches of woods ('are you really sure there's nobody about?'), on the sofa when absolutely everyone was definitely out for the *whole* evening ('and be careful, this cover is brand new'), if all those are included. They may not all have been seen in optimum conditions but in their plurality they would create an idea of the erect cock above and beyond any individual example, just as we know that, say, a chair is not just the ribbed wooden affair with the worn stitched seat in which we happen to be sitting but something to do with every chair we have ever seen and yet also separate from all of them.

So, as Tony's cock expanded in the soft circle of Susan's pulpy lips, I was seeing something for the first time and I found myself intrigued rather than enraged. No individual part of the whole was obviously expanding, the flesh did not appear to be stretching, yet it was always larger than it had been a second or two previously. When Susan lifted herself up dripping and panting to look at her handiwork, I saw that the foreskin had retracted back over the glans and his cock was now capable of sustaining itself at what might have seemed to be a precariously acute angle without sinking down to his stomach. There was a time when I might have felt envious. She was now seated astride him and I was suddenly at the wrong angle to observe her familiar technique of employing the cock as a tool of self-stimulation before impaling herself firmly upon it.

Sexual intercourse of an energetic kind now took place, with all the lights on, and your eighteen-inch anthropologist craning his neck in the corner. It all looked so big and so violent, a vast wasteful manufacturing process. What did I feel as I saw, well, let's not spare myself, Tony's cock ramming in and out of my ex-girlfriend's cunt, until finally it slunk out leaving a snail's trail behind it?

Not as much as you might think. In these pages I have as yet barely touched on the not entirely unhappy but nevertheless disillusioning week that I spent in the enforced company of what I must now call my own kind. There were, including me, eleven monkeys in the large cage, barely distinguishable either by sex or by size. After a day of taxonomic and numerical struggle, repeatedly losing count through my inability to tell my fellow prisoners apart, I was able to establish that there were seven male monkeys and four female. Of an average twenty-four hours, much was spent semi-comatose inside the small shelter at the rear of the cage and the rest consisted of some mutual grooming, to which I was suspiciously and grudgingly admitted, two regular feeds and intermittent bursts of activity which were much applauded by the vast pink balloon faces of the ghouls outside the wire.

Had I anticipated my metamorphosis, I would have assumed the ape's sexual activity to be of a hierarchical, ordered, regimented kind, even allowing for the distortions provoked by their unnatural environment of concrete and cold metal. Reckoning that the female was receptive for, say, five days a month, it might be reasonable to assume that there would be some visible sign of this, and that impregnation would then occur from a male who had established his right to fulfil that function, perhaps through size, ritualized combat or even actual combat. If the conditions of confinement were to have any effect it would be, I would have imagined, to dampen down the procreative urge. I don't suppose pandas are particularly similar to miniature primates, but even I, in my ignorance of the natural world, had heard about the insuperable problems of trying to get one panda on top of another.

This could hardly have been further from the prevailing state of affairs in the monkey house. Either the experience of being locked up for life has warped our behaviour patterns, or a gene lodged in monkeys of my gender and kind has decided that its best chances of survival are by inserting itself into any feasible hole. Whichever is to blame, our only means of courtship, I quickly observed, is to leap on the nearest vulnerable-looking female from behind and cram our small tumescent pricks more or less into her—no problems with impotence on that side of the wire—and try to come as quickly as possible. It is a technique that some women may recognize, the only difference being that human females are meant to pretend they enjoy it, whereas the female monkeys scream and attempt to fend the male off. Once they have decided that there is nothing to be done, they fidget or continue to eat or scratch while the crazed, blind copulation takes its course. On the third day of this intermittent orgy I found myself with a small erection—necessarily, they were all small—and decided to experiment on a female who was curled up asleep in the straw, right out of view of any human spectators. I gingerly pressed myself against her but, frantically search as I did, I was utterly incapable of locating any feasible orifice in this brief window of opportunity.

Meanwhile the young female concerned woke from what must have seemed like a very unpleasant dream and, clearly sensing that she was at the shallow end of the gene pool, turned and lashed out at me with her teeth and claws. With a streak of pain across my face and a throbbing groin, I shambled to the top far corner of the cage.

Life in the cage was largely tedious, even by the undemanding standards of the monkeys themselves. Trapped without vegetation in an unremittingly monotonous landscape with a static population, they spent most of their life gloomily prone in a form of half slumber. I couldn't deny that the monkey life was a considerable improvement on life as I had lived it previously, but I still wanted reading matter, and perhaps an occasional radio or television programme. Shame of shames, I was even reduced to eavesdropping on the lamentable conversations engaged in by the human voyeurs.

Most of these exchanges expressed nothing more than uninformed wonder, anthropomorphic explanations to children and vulgar expressions of disappointment at the failure of the show to appear the way that it did in the real world on television. But there were also sad dramas played out, so that sometimes it seemed as if the world outside were in a cage and we had been brought across the world as tourists, spectators of the strange practices of a lost species. Families, or parts thereof, would try to bridge chasms, not between them and us but between each other, with a helium-filled balloon and a hat shaped like the ears of a giraffe. I would stare from my cage, an audience of one for the biggest show on earth, at the hopeful baffled enthusiasm of humans barely larger than myself accompanied by the trapped boredom of an accompanying parent.

Rape and boredom behind me, rage and boredom before me—how could the *ménage* of Susan and Tony, whatever concomitant torments there might be, not be a respite? Their sexual activity disturbed me, or at least a part of my brain knew that it ought to be disturbed but also realized that to feel actual distress would have been like emerging from an abattoir and fainting at the sight of a hot dog stand. As I watched their huge knotted limbs and heard their cries and groans, strangely deep to me in sound, I thought with horror of a world of copulation, a blind instinctive craving, a yielding of self, reaching right down to the smallest insect, or even bacteria, for all I knew. When they, Susan and Tony, that is, I'm sure the bacteria never stop at all, finally left off, and lay across each other as if they had been dropped from a great height, I felt a relief. I was out of at least that frenzy for ever.

Incidentally, the other undeniable improvement from the days inside was the matter of hygiene. The monkeys were reasonably fastidious, but they lived in a grotesquely insanitary environment, plagued by the appalling smells emanating from the other cages, the rubbish left by the human visitors and above all the inadequate measures taken by attendants to clean our own cage.

The more zoologically minded among you will want to know whether I was house-trained. It is a curious fact that when so much had changed, some of my old inhibitions stubbornly survived. The bowels of my new body had seemed pretty uncontrollable but I did once make an effort to use a lavatory, grasping perilously on to the outer rim of the plastic seat as I projected my hard round turds into the water far below. Of course it was a disaster. My claws slipped on the unyielding plastic and I found myself flying backwards through space, landing wedged in the water at the bottom, surrounded by floating, well, they would have been like raisins in my previous incarnation but were now Christmas puddings jostling together and against their ex-custodian. I shrieked miserably until rescued by Tony, who lifted me out and wiped me down:

'You know, I think Greg's starting to believe that he's a human being,' he concluded his amusing description of the farcical events to Susan on her return from somewhere outside in the world. With an overwhelming self-control beyond my species, I refrained from displaying my command of rudimentary sign language.

V

MY LIFE NOW began to take on a routine. Writing at night, then snoozing, eating and, most important of all, performing during the day. I was always aware that my hosts had no commitment to me. My consumption of fruit and other foodstuffs was not negligible, and I knew that if I started to bore or irritate them, then if I was lucky it would be back to life among the Regent's Park rapists. If I was unlucky it might be a few months forcibly inhaling cigarettes in a government research establishment before having my chest cut open without anaesthetic. My deportment and behaviour were in themselves matters that required constant thought and planning. If they wanted to play, then I would march up and down like a soldier, roll over and play dead, cuddle up like a baby or whatever nauseat-ing behaviour seemed to be required on a particular occasion. If they wanted to watch a video quietly, then that was better still, and I could sit and watch it too, while pretending not to. The only exceptions were foreign films, which I had disliked enough before, but now my new maladapted eyes could barely read the subtitles. In those cases I would go upstairs and read a book.

They even went away for weekends leaving me with a bowl of fruit and I was careful then to shit in the flowerpots in the yard and make just the right amount of mess so that they wouldn't start wondering if something was wrong, if I might be a mutation or a Japanese robot. At first those weekends were my favourite times, allowing me relative freedom to explore. But after two or three such opportunities I surprised myself by discovering that I missed their presence, with all its attendant anxieties. Sometimes one of them would enter the room where I was reading a newspaper, which was like a human having to extract information printed on bed sheets, and I would have to pretend to be cutely flapping it around. On occasions like this I would feel like a double agent operating without respite under the eyes of the enemy.

There was also my darker scheme. My purpose was not to act as an avenging angel punishing Susan and Tony. To be punished is to know you are being punished by someone, and if they thought I had become the instrument of punishment they would interpret it not as punishment but uncontrollability, and I would find myself wrapped up in a plastic bag and left out for the binmen. What I had to create was a very, very subtle version of the book of Job, only with God left out. To create torments whose source they could not trace was not good enough. I had to create torments which they did not even recognize as torments. My difficult task was rather to choreograph a mood in which they would wonder why they felt so depressed, so bitter with each other, such a sense of failure, without there being any apparent cause. I remember the windy night when that thought first formed itself in my mind, and I uttered a low, daemonic, monkeyish cackle.

Painstakingly, with the utmost measures to preserve secrecy, I began to adopt certain habits. One of them was to listen to the messages on the telephone answering machine. I didn't do anything with the information. I always pressed the STORE button afterwards, allowing the messages to be played back as if nothing had happened. But I waited for my moment, like a kingfisher perched on a branch, apparently asleep, awaiting the shadowy glimmer of a minnow. One weekday afternoon, when Susan had left the house briefly and unexpectedly, there was a message on the machine from a harassed Tony:

'Oh, fuck. I really wanted to talk to you. Look I'm really sorry but I've got to do a clinic this evening, so I've had to call off tonight. Look I rang Jim and told him we can't make it and to give the tickets to somebody else. I'm really sorry about this but, look I've got to dash. I'll see you much later. Lots of love. Bye.'

I knew that they were planning that evening to visit an alternative theatre in Hammersmith, a long distance from Camden Town, and a gratifyingly cumbersome and awkward journey, to see a highly praised experimental show that had been brought at great expense from abroad and was sold out for the whole of its very short run. It was perhaps a little insensitive of Tony to dispose of both the tickets, rather than allowing Susan to find someone else to go with her. But that was small potatoes and would, in itself, scarcely have provoked a cross word. At the electric socket I switched the switch off and then I switched the switch on again, thus creating my own personal, small-scale power cut. It was the simplest of matters. The effect of a power cut on this British Telecom model was to cause the machine to flash its lights helplessly, signalling its distress. I had even left Susan with a way out. If it occurred to her that a message might have been left, she could simply play the tape back. But Susan, though practical in many respects, wasn't good with machines and I doubted whether she would think of that way out, as indeed she didn't, and anyway would scarcely have had time to, so early did she have to leave in order to get to Hammersmith to meet Tony and Jim and Sal. That was the neatness of it. There were plenty of other first moves I could have made. An obvious act of sabotage would have been to perform the same trick with Susan's word processor at some time when she had written a lot of text without taking the trouble to save it. The weakness with that possibility was that while it would certainly have provoked anguish and misery, my greater purpose was to stimulate the dissension between her and Tony that would be provoked by my answering machine stratagem.

'You are a fuckwit, you know.'

That was a good start. Though I was surprised that Susan did not come through the door until shortly after midnight. Even with the best efforts of the London Underground service I didn't imagine it would be much after eight that she would burst in, looking for someone to kick, the way she had once kicked me on some trivial provocation. In my human form, that is. She never struck her pet monkey. Tony looked up from the television, innocent of the tempest that I believed was about to strike.

'Where have you been?'

'All the way to fucking Hammersmith and if I hadn't met someone with a return, no thanks at all to the doctor or his hopeless friends, I'd have come straight fucking all the way back.'

'God I'm sorry. Didn't you get the message?'

'What message?'

And that was it. End of row. The first plague of Egypt has been cancelled. Tony then took Susan upstairs and they examined the answering machine. Oh, a power cut. Then he played back the message to a Susan who wasn't all that cross anyway. Look let's have a drink he said in an unctuous tone, which they did and she told him about the play while he half watched the television and then they went upstairs and had a good old fuck, fortunately on this occasion without my being present.

Not a good start. But the next weeks saw an extended game of chess, though one where only one player was aware a game was taking place at all. It was a form of secret war that I can only compare to the use by the Allies of the Ultra machine at Bletchley Park in the Second World War. The Allied leaders were receiving the Germans' most sensitive signals but had to use the information in such a way that the Germans would never suspect that their secrets were being intercepted. Too many or too obvious successes and all would be lost.

VI

DO YOU KNOW that feeling when the little things in your life seem to be going wrong? A cake gets baked with what must have been salt rather than sugar. Somehow the purple T-shirt goes in with the rest of the wash and absolutely everything goes a shade of light blue, but not so definitely light blue that it could be mistaken for the intended colour of the garment. The key, the only key, to the back door just disappears.

Back in the ancient world such a succession of mishaps would have been attributed to the displeasure of a household deity, who would have been placated by the sacrifice of the nearest disposable domestic pet. But my series of manufactured plagues failed to create the fatalistic sense of entropic failure that I had anticipated. In her blacker moods, the Susan that I had met would start to sob uncontrollably if she had poured her cornflakes into the bowl and then discovered someone else had finished the milk. But the trickles of stones that I regularly set off never turned into an avalanche. The cake was thrown away and another one bought and introduced to the guests with a charmingly self-mocking account of what had gone wrong. In the end Tony actually went to an important dinner in a grey-blue dress shirt ('They're all so pissed by half an hour in, I could arrive in a posing pouch and no one would notice'). And the back-door lock was changed and no fewer than four keys obtained:

'Now pay attention. *You've* got one, *I've* got one, there's one in the door and one in the cup on the shelf. When we move we take the door with us.'

At this stage there is another more serious question that will be asked by readers who are truly empathetic with the experience of seeing what it's like when your ex-lover is in love. I asked it of myself late one Saturday evening when we were watching a movie. Tony was sitting on the sofa, Susan was stretched across it with her head in his lap and I was sitting on the arm pretending to play some monkeyish game with a walnut. The film's music and lighting had altered to signal an extended sex scene and I was wondering whether we were really going to see the leading actress's pubic hair—it relied on her dropping her thigh slightly—when I became aware of some activity beside me.

'Have you got an erection? Does she excite you that much? You bloody have.'

'She leaves me completely unmoved.'

Susan opened his fly buttons, inserted her hand and tugged unavailingly. Tony let out a cry.

'Stop, it's trapped, it's trapped, emergency.'

As I have already indicated, my changed state had shielded me from anguish like a local anaesthetic. But anaesthetics are not infallible. I had had bad experiences with them in the many human hours I had spent sitting in dentists' chairs counting the paint bubbles on the ceiling. I would sit in the reassuring fog of numbness, smelling the sweet burning stench of drilled tooth and wondering if the tooth was hurting somewhere where I couldn't feel it, when suddenly the drill would break through on to the nerve and pierce the frail carapace beneath which I was sheltering. The cold metallic liquid of pain would flow through my head back and forwards. Watching Tony and Susan laughing and having sex, that double intimacy, I suddenly remembered once more what pain was like.

They both laughed at the release of Tony's cock, springing up to the level of my head and less than a foot away, and Susan giggled as she took it in her mouth to Tony's theatrical groans, moving up and down its shaft with sudden intensity. More screams and his cock, still in her mouth, went soft; chalky, snotty liquid ran from her lips down into his wiry pubic hair. I felt both interested in every detail and also the sensation of a dull remembered ache in my little belly, rising into my throat and spreading into my jaw and skull. Susan got a tissue, she had to stretch her body to extract it from the tight front pocket of her jeans. Then she gave a flirtatious little moue at nothing and wiped around her lips then quickly and lightly mopped along and around Tony's shrunken cock that now barely peeked over the wrinkled trench top of his underpants.

'You can put it away now. I think I need some tea.'

So this is what it was like to be alive.

The question that the aforementioned empathetic reader may be asking, and which I asked myself as the now baffling film resumed its story, was why didn't I, from my position of safety, simply burn the house down in the middle of the night with Tony and Susan in it, a final flaming act of suttee for my human existence?

I pictured the blaze with red tenders squeezed into the street, neighbours out on the pavement in incongruous dressing gowns, the dripping grey remnants in the morning through which two long plastic bags would be carried by men with professional expressions on their faces. But it was not now in my nature to do this. I was a parasite, and I am using the word now in my capacity as a part of the natural world. My purpose was to live as part of the organism, feeding off it, without actually killing it. And in the parasitical hierarchy, I probably stand quite high. I'm certainly higher than those fish who spend their entire lives hovering round the arsehole of a whale. A good deal higher. As for intestinal worms, there's no television for them and no fruit, at least in an unmasticated form. They're right down off the bottom of the chart.

Was there something humiliating about my situation? A

small animal jocularly named after my former self with the connivance of my ex-lover's new lover, bearing witness to the extent of my disappearance from her life? But in order to be humiliated one must be humiliated in front of someone and who is there for me to fear except for you, the reader? I know Susan now better than I ever did when she and I shared a bed, I know her better than Tony, perhaps better than anyone knows anyone.

As I write these lines—the street light outside has just extinguished itself leaving a grey penumbra that signals the imminence of a feeble dawn and the end of the night's work—my small hand trembles around the pen that I'm painfully clutching and I feel like a traveller who has returned from a strange land. I'm a Neil Armstrong, the first person into a new world. It's not just that I've seen Susan having a shit, something which she would never have permitted another human to witness, and if she had it would have been a performance anyway. But who cares if there's a small monkey in the bathroom? I've seen her heedlessly sitting open-legged on the lavatory, the review section of the paper rustling on her lap, enjoying her own splashes and smells, delicately folding the soft paper and then wiping herself with an abstracted wrinkle of concentration on her brow. Once, deliriously, I saw her put a long fingernail into a nostril, extract a hard remnant of snot and chew on it. This afternoon, Tony being at work, I alone witnessed her vomiting into the lavatory, her gargling coughs amplified by the green porcelain. And I've seen her alone, her face becoming a beautiful hard edged mask, staring through the steam of her coffee, thinking of, what? Me perhaps.

VIII

I LIKE TONY. I knew that of the pair he was the more reluctant to admit me to what was, after all, his home. Since then I have not been notably effective in endearing myself to him with my winsome frolics, my prancing and slapstick. I am tolerated. I am not like the stereo system or the radio. Still less am I like Susan, whatever it is exactly that she is to him. I am like one of the plants, accepted as a part of the environment, demanding a certain level of care, but not something whose company he seeks.

Tony is self-contained, almost self-sufficient, and this is what I like him for. Susan is always restless, making demands on everything about her. She will read a few pages of a book, switch on the television, change channels, rearrange the pots and china on the mantelpiece, make tea, engage Tony in random conversation, put on Part One of a Spanish language course that she owned before I met her, get depressed, wash her hair, slice pieces of banana and throw them at me, wonder aloud why the house is not selling, whether she should give up everything and begin a new career, go to sleep. Meanwhile Tony will have been sitting, stolid as a dark-haired little troll, engaged in a single task, reading one book at a time, taking notes from a paper, or just lying with his eyes unseeing and narrowed at some jagged, jangling Bach sonata.

Occasionally, with the same, almost abstract, sense of purpose he will fetch some fruit from the kitchen and lie on the floor, slicing it carefully over a plate. Once it has been reduced to strips, slices or sections he will solemnly, almost confidingly, feed me, piece by piece, man to man, sometimes sampling the fruit himself, as if to demonstrate politely that he would never serve anything to a guest that he would be unwilling to eat himself. Most mercifully of all, he does not, like some nervously cackling guests, talk to me. Here, Greg. Nice, Greg. Catch, Greg. His courteous gravity signals to me that we have reached some agreement over Susan's life and her body.

What else do I like? There is a sheepskin rug that spends its posthumous life spreadeagled on the double bed. It is my preferred location for a nap and my place of refuge when clumsy, boisterous people invade. I also seek out patches of carpet that glow hot and white in the sunshine during the mornings, and in the evenings there is a corner where a radiator meets the end of the bed. In the summer I climbed the trellis in the yard, the one on the wall that miraculously received sun from mid morning almost until sunset, by which time I was almost stunned by the waves of jasmine scent carrying a suggestion of a life beyond the seas. Then disaster struck and I, even with my small weight, brought it down and the tresses of jasmine with it. I faced the prospect of consignment to the laboratory where shampoo will be dripped on to the stitched-open eye every day from nine till five. There were a few curses, but it was a welcoming morning and Tony not only fastened it up again, but trimmed the jasmine back, repotted a handful of other plants, finally cleared out the planks and plastic sheeting that had been stuffed in the corner ever since he'd moved in, cut back the weeds growing with extraordinary profusion from between the paving stones and all in all had a very satisfying day, so much so that by the time he finally sat down in a deckchair to catch the last of the sun he opulently rewarded me with a cold quarter of melon, himself greedily gnawing the other quarter. We looked at each other with water dripping from our chins.

Of fruit, in general, I am a connoisseur. The perfume-clogged water of melons, the yellow sweetness of mangos that turns bitter at the back of the mouth, the pear's grainy mousse. And then all those lovely leather, plastic, rubber, paper skins that I used to spurn before. However, I am not by design a fruitarian, as my hosts have discovered empirically by tossing me scraps from their table. I have sometimes looked wistfully at the cats that prance thoughtlessly along the high wall. Someone would be sure to miss even one of the tender small ones.

My favourite receptacle in the house is a tiny wooden tub, like an ancient washtub for a doll's house, that Susan keeps on the writing desk in the front room upstairs. It is full of pointless objects: one large screw and two small ones; a picture hook with no accompanying nail; a halfpenny stamp, an opaque marble, a large, square leather button; a rubber for rubbing out ink; one token cut out from a box of washing powder which required six more plus postage by the end of October 1986 to obtain a kitchen towel decorated with the company's logo; one drawing pin, which Tony does not permit to be driven into his wall; and two photographs from a strip of four portraits of Susan taken in an automatic booth. I spent an entire morning delicately removing the items one by one in my perfect little baby fingers, arranging them in groups on the worn green baize and wondering at the conclusion why this had been so satisfying.

And then there is Susan herself, the object of my research. I found it impossible to live without her, but in truth I found it difficult to sleep with her. Like so much in our relationship, I was in love with the idea but had difficulty with the reality. I loved the idea of those nights—there must have been more than three hundred of them—during which we lay for hours, unconscious together. How trusting, to spend all that time, naked and asleep with someone. Sometimes, spurred on by this thought, I wanted to keep my arm protectively around her, but if I lay facing her with my right arm over her trunk, what did I do with the left? The arrangement would only have been bearable for more than a few minutes at a time if there had been a hole in the bed through which I could insert it, or, more comfortable still, if the left arm had been amputated at the shoulder. I generally ended up on my back or pointing away from her. But now sometimes when the words won't come, or my arm aches, I retreat into the bedroom and crawl beneath the duvet into the soft corner between her breast and upper arm. Once, in the first light, I saw a smile pass over her sleepy features. Another time she stirred, gripped me by the ripple of flesh at the back of my neck and tossed me from the bed on to the carpet.

IX

OPEN SESAME. Speak friend and enter. I have been into the magic cave and have returned. All unawares, Susan has let me inside her.

It began badly—for me—with one of those evenings that Susan and I never quite got around to having, in front of the fire, with a couple of bottles of wine and bits of food that hadn't needed much preparation and the two humans of the trio both in their dressing gowns. I crouched soberly on the edge of the segment of warmth observing a comparison of schooldays begin and then culminate in Tony's running upstairs and returning with a large envelope full of school photographs. There was the under-twelve cross country team—Tony was the improbably tiny child right at the back, standing on a bench; the under-thirteen and under-fourteen cricket teams; and the under-twelve, under-thirteen, under-fourteen, under-fifteen, second fifteen and first fifteen rugby teams, each marked by the writing on the oval ball held in the middle of the front row by a bullfrog-chested captain (in the second fifteen it was Tony himself).

Like a film of a growing mushroom in a science documentary, hair grew long and shortened; pimples came and went; an expression of surliness appeared; suddenly and improbably in the last two pictures he sprouted in size, a change that seemed to take even its subject by surprise.

'Now look at this.'

Tony unrolled a photograph that was just six inches high but fully three feet long.

'You see, we sat in a crescent and the camera moved round.'

'I know, and someone at one end could run around and appear at the other.'

'That's the theory but unfortunately I got it the wrong way round and magically disappeared completely from both halves of the picture. No, there I am. I moved a bit.'

Susan put her finger on the tiny smiling blurred face. Tony's finger moved around the scroll.

'That's Paul Richardson. He's dead, on a motorcycle. Jerry Weston. They found him one morning at the bottom of a block of flats. There was never a proper explanation for it—I don't mean it was murder, or anything like that—but we never knew what happened. He was the first boy of my own age that I ever knew who died. That's Mick Manzini and somewhere along here, yes, there, that's something Pollock. I forget his first name. John, I think. They both committed suicide. Long after leaving the school. And that's Fran McKelvey and his older brother Clive is somewhere in the picture. I know one of them died in a car crash but I don't know which one. If I ever see one of them in the street I'll know.'

Tony's finger of fate drifted on top of the sea of grinning faces pausing to identify a drug arrest here, that was the son of a Labour MP; that one used to steal the newspaper from the library and was now in line for a safe Tory seat; an instigator of an abortion there; fame and fortune for one boy, a nervous breakdown for the long-haired beautiful youth beside him. He was in prison, or had been when last heard of, that one had a column in a national newspaper. Then Susan was goaded into producing her own incriminating pictures. She pulled her dressing gown closer around her and ran upstairs two steps at a time. I heard rattling from the back room and then she reappeared, carrying a small armful.

There she was at six sitting at a miniature table, her right arm stiffly placed across a picture, a round-faced called-for smile at the camera with just a whisper, frailer even than the smile, of the girl who was shortly going to go upstairs and fuck Tony. And there she was in the fifth form, unmistakably Susan, already at her full height at the back in the middle with the other gawky tall girls. Tony took the picture and looked at the scrubbed faces, grinning or bored:

'That endangered species, the English virgin,' he said. Susan laughed.

'Where? I don't see one.'

'You're joking.'

'This is the fifth form picture, not the third form.'

'You're joking.'

Susan put her arm round Tony and kissed him, perhaps a bit patronizingly, on the ear.

'Yes, of course, my love.'

They flicked through the other pictures, Susan brandishing a hockey stick, Susan holding a swimming cup—what was that? a lacrosse thing?—but the mood of hilarity had chilled and the pictures were soon abandoned on the carpet. The two watched television for a bit, Susan stroking Tony's hair, then they went to bed. I looked at the pictures of Susan for a few minutes, her smooth hopeful young face wavy red in the glow of the fire. Then a thought came into my mind. I hopped up the stairs, just one step at a time, along the corridor to the spare bedroom. There it was, Susan's treasure chest gaping open, its riches promiscuously open to the air and to the light from the bare electric bulb dangling on a chafed wire.

This old inherited trunk, the sort that people hide bodies in before dismembering them and disposing of the pieces, was the repository of the documentary history of Susan Gower, or rather, all of it that she had allowed to survive. She told me, before the time when she felt that every confidence was evidence which I was taking down and would later use against her, that one boyfriend—called Brian, I had a infallible memory for the names of people who had fucked her—had written a thoughtless, frivolous letter breaking off with her. She had struggled to reply and then instead had thrown away, in heaps carried in relays to the big bin outside, every personal letter she had ever received. This impetuous action would at least save me some time during the night's work, for I had to assume that I would only have seven hours or so before the documents must be back.

There remained certificates of examinations ranging all the way back to one, signed by the Mayor of Camden Council, for swimming one width of a pool in 1961. There were telegrams of acceptance, her finals papers, a letter from her tutor with her finals results, an almost indecipherable conjunction of alphas and betas, but manifestly better than my own stolid lower second, achieved with such effort. But like Columbus setting forth into the unknown on a voyage of discovery, I knew what I was looking for, and I had already for one tantalizing moment held one of the precious volumes in my hands. I had been browsing through her bookshelves and had casually taken down what looked like a worn old scrapbook, just one of several, which on inspection proved to contain familiar handwriting. I asked what it was. Nothing for your eyes, thank you very much, she said, leaning across and whipping it smartly from under my cheated gaze. Under cross-examination she confessed to having kept a diary intermittently since her early teenage years. On hearing that I felt like a heroin addict deprived of his beloved solution. No matter what the cost, I had to see those books. A small and unconvincing voice in my head told me that reading them would be good for our relationship. If you love someone, said the wheedling whine in my inner ear, you quite simply love everything about her and the more you discover about her the more you love her. Isn't that what Rousseau did? Didn't Tolstoy make his new bride—prudently after they were married, of course—sit down and read all his journals covering his earlier philandering existence, and didn't Susan say that *Anna Karenina* was her favourite novel? Perhaps this was a way of finally turning what was frankly a crumbling relationship into something mature based on secure knowledge. And if it didn't do that it would at least be fucking interesting, and there was little enough of that in my life at that time.

On my very next, tremblingly anticipated, visit to the house where she lived I waited until she was distracted and then snuck up to her room. The paper birds were flown and the bookshelf had a missing tooth, an accusatory vacuum of mistrust. I never saw the books again until, lifting aside her life's documentation, I found the neatly stacked volumes, pregnant with secrets, the Susan Gower archive, the holograph edition of the collected diaries of Susan Gower in eight volumes, for the first time under the eyes of their loving editor, introducer, annotator, textual critic and psychoanalyst.

It is not, I should say first, a uniform edition. The first

volume, chronologically, is a small-format book, bound in ribbed, padded plastic, bearing the inscription, AUTOGRAPHS. It also contains, as do various other of the volumes, interleaved pages, written on an assortment of papers, from ruled exercise sheets of the sort readily available in school rooms to heavy notepaper in various pastel shades. The next volume in the series is a cheap paperback, whose cover is adorned by pictures of horses' heads and titled MY BOOK. The next two are yellow-covered exercise books, presumably purloined from school, each cover bearing the handwritten inscription, SUSAN GOWER'S SECRET DIARY—DO NOT READ. Then, one can only assume, on entering the sixth form, Gower had larger scope for her thieving ways, and the remaining books of the series are all hardbacked A4 lined writing books, which had seen her through to her early twenties when her self-memorializing impulse was dissipated by the pressures that then began to dominate her life.

It should not be assumed that these were simply eight volumes full of diary entries from beginning to end, as I had first assumed with some awe. A cursory examination revealed that only one of them was full and only in one other case had Susan reached beyond halfway. In the horse volume she had barely covered a dozen pages. Nor was the text entirely a journal. There were drawings, poems of little biographical interest, and even two short attempts at fiction, one of which I shall return to.

It is in archives like this, in people's hidden drawers, the back of the upper shelves of their cupboards, that the truth about human beings is to be found, their secrets, their fears, their quavering embarrassments, the sins and desires they have not confessed to their most intimate companions, perhaps not even fully to themselves. We ought not to know these things, that X fantasizes about little boys, that Y has holidays on her own where she fucks strange people, that Z once had a mental breakdown but managed to keep it to himself. Human civilization depends on our not knowing these things about each other.

This truth became clear to me as I sat with the volumes. They were so interesting and I'm not human and they seemed, to my distorted vision, to be leaning forward, begging me to open them. Very well. I'll be good, Lord, but first let me look at these volumes. I waited, and suddenly, in the middle of that dark night, I felt a wave of tranquillity wash over me, as if somehow this intrusion had been sanctioned by a higher authority. If I read Susan Gower's journals, her naïve, poignant account of a girl's coming of age, and read them with a pure and forgiving heart, then that would be a fitting farewell to human life.

I opened the first volume.

X

WHEN, AFTER MY necessarily hurried and selective survey, I had read the last page of the final volume, I must confess my emotions were mixed. The diaries were no peephole straight into a young girl's heart. I had expected Susan to recount her sexual coming of age in fresh, unaffected, almost unformed language. But in these pages it was only perceptible in a form distorted and vulgarized by its chronicler's reading of magazines, fiction and poetry. Once the fear and trembling of a first sexual experience has been filtered through Keats, D. H. Lawrence, Charlotte Brontë and the problem pages of a pubescent girls' magazine, the result is sickly and synthetic, a wild flower that has become a cardboard air freshener. It was only through a strenuous act of my redemptive imagination that I was able to get beyond Susan's febrile kitsch to the authentic feeling that lay behind it.

Take that much fetishized subject, the loss of her virginity, which occurred a month after her sixteenth birthday. Susan's steady boyfriend was called Alex. I had in fact once met Alex at a party of an old school friend of Susan's. He was a person of a height so towering—about six feet six, or something absurd like that—that one couldn't quite take it seriously; one wanted to tell him to come down from up there and stop fooling around. He now sold computer software; he had—since Susan's time—lost his eye in a car accident; and he now had a wife and no fewer than three children. His hair was flaming red, his skin was pale and he wore a permanent nervous smile which was generally (I suppose unavoidably) aimed over his interlocutor's head.

However, even at that time, what I knew and he didn't was that he had not been awarded the prize of Susan's virginity. That had gone to Tobe. The description of the encounter is not to be found in the diary itself but in a short story, written on three unlined sheets of typing paper, folded twice and pushed inside the first diary. The edges of the pages that had projected out of their protective hard covers were yellowed, dusty and crumbling, but the text itself was clear enough. Previously, despite certain discreet, apparently uninterested inquiries, I had known nothing about him beyond his slightly sinister name, and the fact that he was the object of Susan's coldly conceived but heatedly executed strategy to dispose of her virginity briskly and without trouble. Unlike Alex, who was only a year older than Susan, and still at school, Tobe was a lad in his twenties, who possessed a car and a flat, and after a party, very early one Sunday morning, he took Susan to the latter in the former.

The account contained some rather ghastly, derivative stuff about stirring of thighs and wetness, but then a nice touch in which her flowerpatterned long dress was thrown back over her head, she felt her knickers slide down her legs, and then, despite struggles with a recalcitrant button at the nape of her neck, her first, very brief, act of sex occurred without her actually seeing it. Tobe was never, as she herself puts it, to become a 'boyfriend' (the quotation marks are hers). Alex was that for the time being, though he was soon accorded what seems to have been a virtually symbolic fuck, described in rather poignantly patronizing style by the now richly experienced woman of pleasure, and sent on his way.

I must not give the impression that the majority of Susan's journals, or even a substantial part, were devoted to her sexual exploits. This was far from the case. From what I could see much of her text was devoted to the common currency of all adolescent life from day to day: accounts of the wearisome routine of school instruction, with occasional holiday breaks; the achieving and forfeiting of female friendships; observations on her reading, her work, her contemporaries; and then—a recurrent topic—much introspective analysis of her own wayward moods. I wondered, while skipping past yet another 'the-world-has-gone-grey' passage (that is a direct quotation from what seems to have been a particularly bad spell), what Susan herself would now make of her journal's self-indulgence, affectation, sentimentality and melodrama. I say this because I myself once kept a journal. It was during my first year at university, and on rereading it several years later, I was so repelled by the grotesque spectre that emerged from the pages with its absurd posturing and self-pity, that I tore the whole thing out of the book, page by page. I suspected as I read that if Susan had had a proper look through her own life, she would not have stored it with such care.

But it was the sexual episodes that I concentrated on during this privileged night. This was not just prurient curiosity, a remnant of the grasping possessiveness that had destroyed our relationship. Sex is the weak point, the fissure where we can break through all the disguises and get at the truth about life. We live in a superficial world of habit, convention and reflex, engaging with people we barely notice. Occasional events, perhaps an accident, a tragedy, force us to see our life freshly. Notice how even after a small injury to, say, a hand, you suddenly have to think about what it means to manipulate objects, to pick things up, to put things into your mouth. Death is the extreme example. On the day I heard that my grandfather had died, when I was eleven, I looked at people in the street and wondered how they could carry on walking around looking so normal when at their age they must know, they must really know, that people suddenly die and we never see them again. In a similar way, sex and the impulses associated with it break through our habitual, unthinking behaviour. Like the cracks in the side of a volcano, revealing the inconceivable white heat beneath, it shows us another world that we skate across, of undirected desire and instinct.

Of course it was curiosity as well, and tantalizing regret. Where was Tobe, the man with the ridiculous name, now? He would be in his late forties, stuck behind a desk, and now he would be called Toby or Mr something. His collar would be too big, his hair would be combed carefully across his head; he would spend his time looking wistfully at the young girls staying the same age while he receded from them. Perhaps he was dead, impaled on the cracked steering column of that enabling car, a day or ten years after vanishing from Susan's life. I envied him, and the cuckolded Alex for that matter, their encounters with her young body. It would have been firmer then, probably; unwrinkled around the breasts, the eyes; just a few years removed then from those mysterious games of hopscotch and jumping over ropes. She would still at that time have been wearing a uniform, and had teachers telling her to behave.

The documentary record of Susan's sex life was, like the fossil record, incomplete. The best that I could do to reconstruct it was as follows. After the enforced departure of Alex into obscurity, she was loosely linked to Francis, who was in his year off and then the first year of university, for the remainder of her school career. This was only interrupted by a turbulent summer holiday between her lower and upper sixths which included brief encounters during a holiday in Greece with Rick, the elder brother of a school friend, and Chas.

I was able to find no journal covering Susan's own year off, which I knew to have been mainly spent as an operative in a central London travel agency. The principal perk of the job was an extended trip to the United States over the summer. The relationship with Francis continued in a hopeless sort of way at university, though the two of them were hundreds of miles apart. There then followed a period of experimentation involving one-, two- or even three-night stands with fellow undergraduates: Pat, an actor; a nameless figure who materialized just once in the aftermath of a party and then disappeared forever; David, an aspiring writer; George, a drug dealer whose already loose connection with the university was severed by his death announced in a later volume of the diary; and Chris, who, on the evidence of Susan's diary entries, seemed to possess no attributes at all apart from a permanent girlfriend with whom he had no intention of breaking up.

There then followed what seemed to have been an intense relationship with Brian, an Irish medical student who was in the first stages of the multiple sclerosis that was—and this I also knew already—to force him into a wheelchair and then slowly strangle him to death. I was able to contemplate Brian with equanimity, even in the passages where for the first time Susan spoke the language of sexual pleasure as well as the routine terminology of love which she had used automatically throughout. Susan took the first term of her second year off for medical reasons and only resumed the following January.

At about this stage in her adventures I became fatigued and dazed, partly by the lateness of the hour and the strain on my eyes of her handwriting, but also by the relentless profusion of the names that came at me like swooping birds. There was Robert, Willie, some hopes unfulfilled from an affair with Jake that was terminated when he went back to the States; Denis, another Tony, Don, who in fact was a don, married with children and who seems to have been the ruin of yet another term. I became repelled by the amnesiac ease with which Susan would once more crank up the rhetoric of first love. And then all that grief, those nights of crying, followed absurdly by the conviction that things would now be different.

Did the journals reduce Susan in my eyes? Yes, they did. She emerged from that long evening like an aged battered freighter encrusted with gravelly barnacles, dragging a chaos of seaweed and clogged, snagged nets behind her. I had at times felt guilty about the effect I had had on her, but was I any worse than the unsavoury crew she had careered between in her earlier life? At least I had stayed around, like dry rot perhaps, but I was there. If not a therapeutic success at solving problems that had been provoked by others, I was at least better than the dismal standard that had prevailed before me.

In the year or so after she left university the journals faltered and finally subsided altogether into a series of scarcely intelligible jottings, some dated, some not, that seemed to extend right up almost to the present. I searched for a report on our unhappy partnership but I found nothing except the final entry in the final book which seemed more like an epitaph than an entry in a diary. She had written the single malformed question: 'I like myself why should I be made to hate myself?' Perhaps she was doing something else at the same time, talking on the phone or something, because around that question she had doodled a jagged frame of triangles and stars, some shaded in so hard that she had worn right through the paper and stained the page below.

Dawn had broken, and I was disturbed from my scrutiny by the sound of the bedroom door opening. The lavatory flushed, and then Susan, her eyes narrowed, her face pummelled out of shape by sleep, appeared in the doorway to find me gambolling merrily among her papers, flinging them around.

'Greg, you naughty thing, what have you been up to? Come here, my darling.' And she picked me up and carried me lovingly back to bed where she fell asleep holding me against her huge white warm heaving body.

XI

THAT MORNING WAS grey with ominous promises of winter. Tony overslept and ran out of the house, hastily and crossly, for the hospital, leaving Susan asleep. She awoke late and dawdled her way through the morning. She had a long steamy bath, her hair pinned up, her breasts cheerfully buoyant. She read a paperback folded double as if it were a magazine, occasionally using her feet to release cooled water through the plughole and then refill the bath from the hot tap. As the bathwater finally turned in on itself and disappeared, she stood in the bath and smilingly rubbed herself dry—her arms, gently round and under her breasts, her tummy, between her legs and over her pubic hair until it ceased to glisten, then with a rough affection down the length of her thighs and calves and between her toes, as if this morning she wanted to prolong the attention she was giving herself.

She stood naked before the mirror, steam still rising from her, and appraised what she saw. Gently she moved the palm of her right hand down the flat of her tummy.

Apparently approving of the result she then quickly dressed herself in jeans, a white tennis shirt, a dark blue sweater and training shoes with no socks. Downstairs she considerately, if unnecessarily, peeled me a banana, then ate breakfast—both halves of a grapefruit eccentrically kept in the fridge, several slices of toast roughly spread with the greasy butter that had been left out overnight and with jam noisily scraped from the bottom of the jar, and a pot of coffee. She picked up the newspaper from the doormat but left it unread on the table. When she had eaten enough she refilled her large rustic-style coffee mug, gathered up yesterday evening's photographs and took them upstairs to the back room.

As a result of my deceptive rummagings, the contents of the trunk were a mess, and Susan did not replace the photographs. Instead she lifted all the papers from the trunk and began the long task of ordering and replacing them. Photographs went in one pile, certificates in another, diaries in another. Yet another was reserved for the rubbish that had inexplicably been preserved: brochures, plastic bags, notices from school, a prospectus for a university she hadn't even attended, a prospectus for the university that she had attended.

Gradually the papers were stacked and returned to the trunk until only the diaries remained. She gathered up the waste paper and her stained coffee mug and descended, returning five minutes later with yet another steaming mug of coffee balanced on an ashtray. She sat back against one wall—I was bouncing a brazil nut against another—lit a cigarette and began to read through volume one, the autograph album. Susan's countenance was of the expressive kind. Even her normal reading face, which she assumed whether she was reading P. G. Wodehouse or the back of a cereal packet, was like a caricature of concentration, her brow furrowed like corrugated iron, her eyes set in a frown of intense thought that was frequently mistaken for a species of anguish. As page after page was turned and she moved from book to book, the expression was maintained, occasionally turning into a faint smile or a look of puzzlement. Once she wiped her eye, at another moment she gave a deep breath and put the book down, her face entirely blank.

At length, after an hour's perusal, she slammed the final book shut with an almost pantomimic sigh—of relief? disgust?—and tossed it on top of its fellows. I ran across and with what I hoped was an endearing gaiety began to scratch at its cover.

'Careful, my darling Greg,' she said, and almost lovingly placed the books one by one into the trunk. As she shut it up I caught a glimpse of one of the dull red covers, for the last time, I was sure. She gave me a good-natured prod out of the door on to the landing:

'Come on, Greg. Work time.'

XII

MY INTEREST IN anything that happens outside these walls, or, with certain exceptions, within them, diminishes daily, but I am aware that I am now attended to by two doctors instead of just one. A hundred thousand or so cigarettes later, Dr Gower finished the thesis that she was never going to finish and so there now exists another contribution to scholarship, another bound volume in that great oblivious library of the unread.

These are the last pages that I shall write. It is not that my manuscript is complete, or that there is not considerably more space remaining in the generous refuge provided by Sir Walter's great work. Over the past days I have reread my thoughts and reflections and, right or wrong, magnanimous or mean spirited, they seemed nothing more substantial than a dream from which I have now almost fully awoken. How could I have cared so much about the insignificant trappings of mortality, things which were anyway irretrievably gone from me? Let them remain in their hiding place, taking their chance, until the day of judgement, a move of house or, least likely of all, a return into fashion of the works of the Laird of Abbotsford. Perhaps there will be a helpful television series.

Over the expanse of time since I last painfully put pen to paper I have put away my foolish mortal thoughts of revenge. Far from regretting my state, I realize that I am in Eden, or more than that, that I have created my own Eden, and that my transformation was no renunciation but a transcendence. The paradise I have forged for myself is decisively superior to that inhabited by the first parents of my former self. There is no forbidden fruit. Apples, pears, grapes, oranges, grapefruit, mangos, kiwi fruit, clementines, tangerines, satsumas, strawberries, cherries, nectarines, peaches and other exotic varieties that supermarkets now increasingly stock are all provided for me in profusion.

Then, transcending all of this, I consider it two paradises in one to be in paradise by myself. I have no primeval Eve to share my burden. There is no one to be jealous of, to wrangle with, insult, ignore, ingratiate myself with, seduce, and the rest of it. All that complication, all that mess is behind me. And to multiply my paradises once more, I do not have the misfortune to be presided over by a single jealous god, mindful of my social fulfilment, devising cruel tests and craving attention in order to divert himself from his own loneliness. Unlike Adam and Eve's lonely and grudging derelict, sulking in the hyperthermic bedsit of the universe, I have two deities, who are all in all to each other, and can survive well enough without my services. There are no demands placed between us, no conflict, barely anything that could be described as a relationship. Merely food and warmth travelling in one direction and nothing in return. I have forgotten how to talk. I pray that soon I shall have forgotten how to write and then how to think, that unnecessary rattling in the skull.

There is, of course, a serpent in Eden, there always must be, a serpent of the old familiar kind. There is a new household deity imminent. Will it expel me from my garden? See how Susan already worships it. Each bright morning in her joy she kneels before the lavatory, bends her face over it and empties her body.